the CHOSEN PATH

the CHOSEN PATH

By Deborah Joyner Johnson

MorningStar Publications
A DIVISION OF MORNINGSTAR FELLOWSHIP CHURCH

P.O. Box 440
Wilkesboro, NC 28697

The Chosen Path
Copyright © 2003 by Deborah Joyner Johnson.

Distributed by MorningStar Publications
A Division of MorningStar Fellowship Church
P.O. Box 440, Wilkesboro, NC 28697

International Standard Book Number 1-929371-27-6

MorningStar's website: www.morningstarministries.org
For information call 1-800-542-0278.

Unless otherwise indicated, all Scriptures are from the New American Standard Bible.

Cover Design by Micah Davis & Tim Dahn
Book Layout by Micah Davis
Map Drawing by Deborah Joyner Johnson
All rights reserved.
Printed in the United States of America.

Table of Contents

Dedication   vii

Foreword   ix

Preface   xi

Part I   ✳   The Calling   13

Part II   ✳   Preparing for the Journey   33

Part III   ✳   The Journey Begins   63

Part IV   ✳   The Journey   109

Part V   ✳   The Great War   165

Part VI   ✳   The Journey Continues   195

Part VII   ✳   The Journey's End   225

Dedication

This book is lovingly dedicated to the courageous
who are pursuing their destiny by following
God's chosen path for their lives.

To my children, Matthew, Meredith, and Abby:
May you find your chosen path and follow it,
drawing ever closer to the King who loves you so much.

To my brother, Rick:
My deepest gratitude for your help and insight, and for
the encouragement to persevere and finish *The Chosen Path*.
Thanks for being such a wonderful big brother!

To all those who helped make this book a reality:
My sincerest and heartfelt thanks.
May God bless each of you
a hundredfold for your faithfulness.

Foreword

The Chosen Path is a captivating story but much more than a story—it is truth. It is written to impart courage and resolve in those who are faithfully committed to the highest of callings.

This book was written especially for the emerging generation. It is now apparent that this generation will not settle for the form of Christianity that dominates much of the church today. The coming generation is addicted to adventure and to the supernatural. Both of these are found in their purest form in the true Christian life. True Christianity is reemerging and passionate souls are finding it. They are the ones who feed on writings like *The Chosen Path.* DO NOT READ THIS AS FICTION—READ IT AS A CALL.

Debbie is my younger sister, and I have watched throughout her life as she has persevered, turning many struggles into victories just as the heroine of this book does, finding her own way to her ultimate purpose. Such experience is always the best source of truth and is the reason why the Lord chose men to write His eternal truth rather than angels. Truth that is living must come through a life. Truth that is life is not just a concept but an experience. The energy that flows through this book is just such a living truth. However, its real message is more than just the reading of a great story—it is the call to live a great story of your own.

When Jesus sent out the disciples to preach the gospel, they returned to Him rejoicing at how even the demons were subject to His name. His reply was that they should rejoice that their names were recorded in the Book of Life (see Luke 10). This is your call, your purpose for being on this earth—to write your own story in the Book of Life that will be an eternal memorial to the love of God, and the power of that love.

The symbolism and metaphors in this story are unashamedly Christian. True Christian life is the ultimate quest and the greatest adventure that can be lived on this earth. It is also the most difficult life that can be lived on this earth, which is why the Lord plainly states that cowards will not be found in His kingdom (see Revelation 21:8).

The Chosen Path is a call to leave the comfortable and secure to pursue the greatest treasure there is—a life that succeeds in fulfilling its purpose—a life that concludes victoriously with the highest reward in all of creation, to hear from the King of kings, "Well done My good and faithful servant!" This is your quest and this book is food for your journey.

Rick Joyner

Preface

There are many paths to choose in life and each will lead to a different outcome. The wisdom to choose the right path is one of the most valuable possessions we can have. This is a story about a girl named Zoe, the path she chooses to follow, and the consequences of that choice. Along the way, she is faced with many other choices, and each holds the power to change her life. It is my hope as you follow Zoe on her life-changing journey that you will grow in this wisdom as well.

The King of kings has already chosen the path for you to follow because of His love for you. More than anything else it will be your love for Him that will enable you to choose the right path which will dictate the course of your life. This path always leads to Him, and to the fulfillment of the purpose for which you were created. As you read about Zoe, I pray that the Lord will clarify your own unique destiny, and that His wisdom will always light your path.

Deborah Joyner Johnson

You will make known to me the path of life;
In Your presence is fullness of joy;
In Your right hand there are pleasures forever.
Psalm 16:11

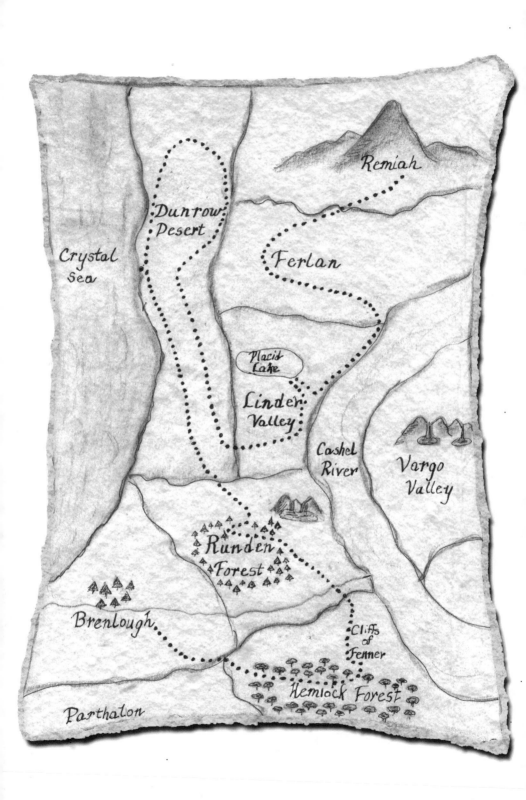

Part I
The Calling

Chapter One

"You whom I have taken from the ends of the earth,
And called from its remotest parts,
And said to you, 'You are My servant,
I have chosen you and not rejected you.'"
Isaiah 41:9

*Z*oe *stared into the distance not daring to breathe, afraid*
that it would all disappear. A man was with her. "What
do you see?"

Still looking far away she replied, "A place more beautiful
than I could ever imagine."

He smiled when he saw the longing in her eyes. "It is possible
for you to go there…" Her gaze left the land as she looked at the
man in hope.

He added simply, "There is a way."

Those were always the last words in her dream. Zoe replayed
the dream over and over in her mind trying to remember if the
man had told her how to find that magnificent land, but it was all
to no avail. She went outside and sat by the stream to think.
She recalled the surprising conversation she had overhead just
yesterday between a man and woman about a land far beyond the
Crystal Sea. They called it Remiah and said that a friend had gone
there. It was a place so beautiful that it seemed like a fantasy—
where peace and freedom filled the land. She could not help but
to think it sounded just like the place in her dream. If so, she

wanted more than anything to go there. Throwing pebbles into the water, she realized that she had never done anything adventurous in her life. Little did she know that by sunset, all that would change dramatically.

Time slipped away. Zoe felt hungry so she walked the well-trodden path to her little stone cottage. When her mind was preoccupied, she had a tendency to forget about food, as her small frame revealed. With delicate features, golden brown eyes, and a glowing complexion from the many hours she spent outside, she was a rare beauty indeed—a fact of which Zoe was totally unaware.

As Zoe approached her cottage, she stopped at the rose garden to inhale the fragrant blooms. Looking around, she admitted this was the first place that ever seemed like home. She liked it here but deep inside she knew there had to be more to this life she lived. She could not let go of the feeling.

Inside, the aroma of porridge simmering over the fire made her mouth water. She quickly scooped a large bowl full and sat down to eat, when there came a knock at the door. She peered out the window to discover a strange man dressed in peculiar clothes, nothing like the clothes the people in the village of Brenlough wore. When Zoe looked at his face, her heart nearly stopped. It was the man from her dream! He even had the same wild white hair and sheepskin clothing. He knocked again. She hesitated opening the door, but curiosity overcame her apprehension—she just had to know who he was and what he wanted.

She bit her lip determined not to show her fear as she cracked the door. "Good day," he said with a smile. "I am Kieran, messenger for the King. Are you Zoe Newbridge?"

Her brow furrowed, as she nervously twirled her long brown curls. "Yes I am."

"I have something for you from the King." He held out a neatly wrapped brown parcel with an envelope attached to the front.

Puzzled, her eyes widened as she opened the door a bit more and took the package. "From the King—for m…me?"

"Yes, I have traveled a great distance to deliver this to you."
He noticed that she seemed uncomfortable and he smiled again.

She looked down at the envelope attached to the box and
rubbed her fingers across the mountain emblem sealed in wax.
Shuffling her feet she asked, "What is this about?"

He grinned. "Do you want to go to Remiah?"

Her eyes widened in disbelief, "Remiah?"

The messenger patiently replied, "Where the King lives."

Her eyes shone with a trace of hope. "I have heard stories about
Remiah and you are saying that it truly does exist?"

"Most assuredly—all live in peace there for our King leads
with justice and He gives freedom to all. There is no sickness or
death in Remiah because love exists in its highest form, and love
is stronger than death. Here you have an enemy who seeks to
destroy by inciting continual conflict, but he has been banished
from Remiah. Harmony and goodwill rule in every living thing
from the grass to the flowers, from the animals to the people."

"Can there really be such a place that we can travel to from
here?" Zoe asked, hardly able to absorb all that the messenger had
said.

Kieran smiled and nodded with such surety that Zoe felt herself starting to believe. He then continued, "I am not at liberty to
disclose everything concerning your quest, but I can say this. If
you decide to make this journey, you will be changed. If you succeed, no longer will fear control you as it has so many times in the
past, but you will live your life in peace and you will be used to
bring peace back to this place."

"I don't think fear controls me as you say. I live alone quite
peacefully."

"If that is true, why is it that you do not venture far from home?"

Zoe stared at the man briefly. "How do you know this?"

"I am a messenger of the King, and He knows all things. He
knows you like no one else does."

"But how can this be? I have never met the King."

"You will understand if you decide to make this journey."

She weighed the invitation carefully. Kieran expected her to go in faith to a place she had only seen in a dream and overhead people talking about—if it was indeed the same place. How could she know for certain if it truly existed?

As if he knew what she was thinking, he said, "You must search your heart. You will find the answer deep within you."

Zoe looked at the stream in front of her house. She suddenly realized she could waste her life daydreaming or go on this quest. But then again, why leave the comfort of her nice little home to go on this journey into the unknown? She weighed those thoughts. "Will you give me a day to think about it?"

"Yes. I'll return tomorrow morning for your answer." As he turned to leave he stopped and looked deeply into her eyes. "While making your decision, do not let fear control you. Once it does, you will be trapped in a life of regret. I can assure you that if you will just begin this journey, the King will help you."

The messenger, looking at her even more intently said, "Do you know what your name means Zoe?"

"Why, no. I've never really thought about it."

"Your name means *life*. The King wants you to have an abundant life and a new life at the same time. You've always felt like there must be more to your life than merely existing, haven't you?"

"Well, yes. I mean, I've always wanted to go places and see new things. I stay so much to myself—sometimes I deeply desire to do something else…" Her eyes wandered away dreamily. "I've just never known what it was, that is until I had the dream."

"There is *so* much more for you Zoe, but it will take faith to begin this new life and great courage to continue." Kieran smiled reassuringly. "I would like to stay and talk longer, but I must leave you now since I have far to travel. I will return tomorrow for your answer." With those words, he turned quickly and left Zoe standing in wonder.

She quietly went inside and sat down in her favorite old blue chair. The springs squeaked every time she moved, but the

familiarity was inviting. She lit a candle and carefully opened the
envelope, cautiously sliding the letter out.

My Dear Zoe,

*You are invited to come to My kingdom, Remiah. I have prepared
a map with a chosen path on which you must travel.*

*You must remain steadfast on this path that will guide you to Me.
Your journey will be dangerous and many of My enemies will try to stop
you, so you must be vigilant as you travel. The risks are great, but if you
prevail and complete your course, the rewards will be far greater.*

*Along the way, you will meet friends who will help you. Embrace them
and learn from them.*

Your King

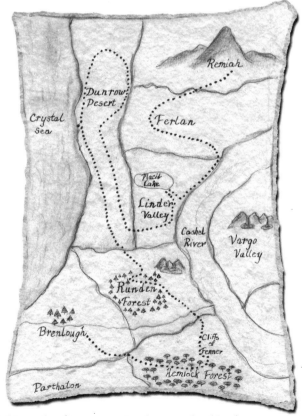

*Taking the first step is always the hardest
but by far the most significant.*

Chapter Two

I pray that the eyes of your heart may be enlightened,
so that you will know what is the hope of His calling,
what are the riches of the glory of His inheritance in the saints,
and what is the surpassing greatness of
His power toward us who believe.
Ephesians 1:18-19

Zoe read the letter several times, making sure she had correctly understood all that was written. The invitation appeared to be genuine. Suddenly excitement filled her heart and she leapt from her chair ready to accept this quest—then just as suddenly, she stopped short when she considered the potential dangers.

Her fearful thoughts were interrupted when she realized that she had not opened the package the King sent. She eagerly tore off the brown paper, and pulled two long dresses out of the box—an unexpected surprise. Her excitement was mixed with disappointment however, because of the color of the dresses. They were the dullest purple she had ever seen. Upon closer examination she could see that they were both the same simple style but one was made out of wool and the other cotton. She slipped the cotton dress over her head and found it was a perfect fit and length, to her ankles just as she liked.

When she took the dress off, it turned inside out. As she looked closer, she discovered a pocket on the inside bodice of the dress. *What a strange place for a pocket,* she thought. Next, she found a tan leather book. A journal to write down her adventures she guessed—she had never owned anything so beautiful and she knew it would be something she would treasure.

Folded inside the journal was a faded map that revealed a path cutting through a terrain of forests, cliffs, a huge desert, a sea, caves, a river, waterfalls, pastures, and then to the mountains where the King lives. Even with the map to guide her, she wondered about the possibility of finding Remiah because of the skill and courage it would take to cross precisely over so many landmarks. What about all the strange creatures she had been told inhabited the lands beyond Brenlough? Still, she could not deny her deep yearning to go to Remiah. Something seemed to be drawing her there.

She looked in the box again and found a crystal bottle. When she opened the bottle, she discovered it was filled with water. Water would definitely be necessary on her journey, so she was thankful to have even a small container to keep it in. At the very bottom of the box was a sturdy brown leather bag to carry everything she needed. She carefully packed all the items into the bag and sat down in her chair. This day seemed like one of her many daydreams.

Zoe's stomach rumbled, breaking the silence to remind her that she still needed to eat, but food was far from her thoughts. Her eyes drifted around her little home, and she saw the dying embers in the fireplace. She wondered if her life would be like those embers, slowly losing life until she died.

For hours doubts plagued her mind. She was too unsettled to eat and it was getting late, so Zoe decided to go to bed. Lying in bed she remembered she had heard of people traveling beyond Brenlough and just disappearing. *Could they have been on their way to Remiah?* She shuddered to think of that, but she *had* received an invitation and the messenger seemed authentic. And what about her dream? It was just a dream—but it seemed so real. Is Remiah the place where dreams become reality? An adventure was what she genuinely desired, but here in her little cottage she was so safe. She had a wonderful and secure life, why should she risk it? All of her insecurities flooded her mind at once. It felt as if they would surely win as she continued to toss and turn for several hours.

She knew that she was facing the biggest decision of her life. Remiah, if indeed it was the place of her dream, promised ultimate peace, life, and security, but to get there seemed like nothing but danger and uncertainty.

Finally, and to her delight, Zoe found herself slowly becoming free of all her worrisome thoughts. It was not long before she was dreaming about a peaceful land far, far away. When she awoke the next morning she was sure of her answer.

Zoe was waiting when the messenger knocked. Again, her fears and doubts came in waves, but the gold flecks in her large brown eyes lit up with pure anticipation as she opened the door for him.

"I will go." She laughed as she repeated herself. "I will go."

Kieran was visibly pleased. "The choice to make this journey was not an easy one for you, but you will not regret this decision, Zoe. Adventures that you have only dreamed about will now be yours. They will bring you life, and you will live more in the next year than most people experience in their lifetime. These adventures will make you into the one you were created to be so that when you arrive in Remiah you can take your intended place. That is your calling, but, as you have been warned, this journey will be quite challenging, and is intended to remove those who lack the faith and courage necessary to reach Remiah, and to reign with the King."

"Sir, I am but a poor commoner. If I can even safely arrive in Remiah, it is far more than I would ever expect to accomplish. But to reign with the King—that is a bit beyond my belief."

"Your faith will grow. From the time of your decision to make this journey you were no longer a commoner, but at this time neither are you the royalty to which you have been called. Even so, you must now begin to think and conduct yourself as one who is called to reign with the King," he said, bowing low before her.

Zoe felt embarrassed, and she knew that her face was very red. Still, a thrill went through her that caused her to stand a little taller. Then the messenger continued, with an obvious respect in his voice that she had not noticed before, which caused her to listen even more carefully to what he was saying.

"The King has many enemies, so when they find out you are going to Remiah, they will try to stop you. They don't want anyone to get close to the King. They are desperate to keep you from achieving your destiny. Do not fear—just walk forward and do not turn back. This is most important, for if you do turn back, the enemy will be waiting with a deadly trap. The King will help you as long as you stay on course. Tomorrow begins a whole new life for you Zoe. Begin your journey as the sun rises. Remember, you cannot fail if you do not stop. Just as it has taken faith for you to begin, it will take increased faith every day for you to continue. Remember that faith will be even more important to you than food."

Faith is the light and guide on every journey.

Chapter Three

"For I know the plans that I have for you," declares the L ORD,
"plans for welfare and not for calamity
to give you a future and a hope."
Jeremiah 29:11

The map revealed that Zoe's first destination would be Hemlock Forest. Not only was the forest filled with the worrisome, hemlock plants, she was also alarmed because of the tales she had heard about that forest. Angry wolves and huge bears were supposedly rampant there. But that was not the worst thing about the forest—it was rumored to be enchanted! Evil creatures were said to constantly roam to and fro throughout the forest, never finding rest or peace. Reportedly, such deep darkness penetrated the forest that one could barely see how to walk—even in the daytime. The longer she looked at the map, the more hesitant she became about venturing into the forest. *Why does the path have to go through that awful place?* But the invitation from the King said she had to travel on the path He had chosen. Clearly, she had no choice but to walk through the forest.

She sighed, put the map inside her bag, and looked around her home for what she expected to be the last time. She smiled in satisfaction for she was very proud of her little stone cottage. Her eyes roamed to her favorite chair where she did her sewing…the little stone fireplace where she prepared her meals…the handmade quilt on her bed…how she would miss this place.

Everything was packed and ready to go. *Am I ready?* She could not deny the yearning inside to go on this journey, so before fear could cause her to change her mind and stay in the safety of her home, she went outside, closed the door, and walked briskly toward the path.

She could not help but turn around and look one last time. She looked at her vegetable garden which was producing so many vegetables that she had had to give most of them away—the majority to the women she sewed for. *Oh my, what am I to do about my customers?* Fortunately, she was caught up on her work, but what would they think when they brought more sewing and she was not at home? She decided to leave a note on the door telling them that she would contact them upon her return. She walked to the stream one last time, where she spent many hours dreaming of distant adventures while gazing at the water—now she was finally on her way.

As she walked away from her home, Zoe turned, found the chosen path, and began her journey. She passed a few cottages, but it was the flowers that captured her attention along the way. For what seemed liked miles, tulips were in bloom, looking like myriads of red, yellow, and purple jewels as the sun's rays shone on the dew that covered them. She was really enjoying herself!

Then in the distance she saw it—Hemlock Forest. She tried to breathe deeply and stay calm, but with every step she took she felt more and more uneasy. By the time she reached the edge of the forest, she was feeling sick with fear. A great battle was raging inside of her. She knew if she turned back she would always wonder—always have a deep regret. She would be safe, but would she really be living?

She decided that a life of regret would be far worse than a walk through the forest. If she was ever to truly live, she had to keep pressing on. Despite her fears, Zoe gathered strength, took a deep breath, and walked forward into the gloomy forest.

She immediately noticed coffee-colored mushrooms protruding everywhere from the moss-covered ground. Creepy vines hung from the trees like webs that were ready to capture their victims. Poisonous, flowering hemlock plants were everywhere. She would certainly stay clear of those deceptive-looking plants.

The cold dampness that enveloped the forest began to penetrate her bones. Her fears suddenly magnified when she heard strange noises all around her, like footsteps falling. She was too scared to even look. Should she run or just keep walking? Zoe remembered the promise of the King's messenger that she would not fail if she did not stop. She decided to risk all on the truth of those words.

As she walked deeper into the woods, she was surprised that nothing grabbed her from behind. The sound of footsteps faded into the thick blackness. But then, the dreaded darkness fell and the eerie silence unnerved Zoe even more than the footsteps. Suddenly, her face and hair were covered with a huge spider web, and inspite of her quick reaction she was entangled! Immediately, a monstrous, black spider jumped on her. She screamed as she felt it crawling on her back, yet she could not reach it. In hysterics, she jumped up and down trying to knock it off, but to no avail! At last, she found a stick and managed to fling the spider away. Tears ran down her face as she frantically began to remove the tangled mess. Heart pounding, she plopped down on a fallen log trying to calm herself. *And this is just the beginning!*

After taking some deep breaths, she remembered her dream, set her determination toward Remiah, and started walking again. The gloomy darkness of the forest enveloped and stifled her. She could see shadows in front of her as she walked—they haunted her with every step she took. Without warning, another large, darker shadow swooped down in front of her, then behind her. Fear she had never known before claimed her and she could barely walk. Then she heard voices, murmurings that she could not understand, yet felt them seep into her very soul filling her with terror. The fear grew to such intensity that she knew she had to get out of this horrid forest! Nothing was worth this.

She turned back toward the entrance of the forest and ran as hard and fast as she could, hearing only the sound of her own panicked breathing. She cried for the opening of the forest. Then she heard noises behind her. At first they were distant, but quickly grew closer until they surrounded her. The darkness reached for her and the wind whistled all around as if it was trying to engulf her. Without warning, two squirrels ran across the path right in front of her, causing her to trip. She realized suddenly what she was doing.

Zoe could not give up this easily. She knew what she had to do. She mustered all the determination she had, turned around, and began resolutely walking back on the path. As she walked deeper into the forest, she heard another noise which was growing in intensity. It sounded like distant drums moving toward her, beating louder and louder as it approached. She gasped as she realized the noise was getting closer and closer. Now it sounded like a herd of animals running toward her. She looked all around and thought she saw the tail of an animal running beside her. Her light brown eyes darkened as they widened with fear, and her heart was beating so loudly that she could hear it! She felt like they were right behind her so she spun around. And then she saw them—a pack of wolves. She nearly fainted with fright and she froze. There was no escape!

The dark gray wolves stopped running, stared at her, and then started creeping closer, snarling and growling, baring their teeth as they encircled her. Their deep blue eyes seemed to be slits of evil. She did not know what to do. If she ran, they would surely catch her! If she stayed where she was, they would attack her. She had to do something, but what? One wolf was so close to her that she could smell his rank breath. His eyes reflected a foulness that she had never seen before—she knew any second she would feel his fangs.

Her tears were spent. Dizziness was causing her to sway back and forth. Her legs and arms began to feel like rubber. Then she felt herself falling to her knees, unable to hold herself up any longer.

The wolves started moving in closer, ready to pounce on their prey. Then suddenly an arrow hit a tree next to her, narrowly missing the nose of one of the wolves. In a haze, Zoe turned to see where the arrow came from and saw a woman step out of the darkness. She shot again and grazed the leg of the largest wolf. When he cried in pain, the rest of the wolves began growling at the woman. Hatred manifested in their eyes as they still kept coming toward Zoe. The woman quickly shot her bow again and hit another wolf in his leg. He yelped in pain and fear came to the faces of the other wolves. Swiftly they turned and disappeared into the woods as quickly as they had appeared.

Zoe lay crumpled on the ground, and the woman ran to her. She lifted her head, and after a few minutes, Zoe awoke. "You gave me a dreadful fright, you did—poor, wee lass. How would you say you're feeling now?"

Zoe looked at the woman who was kneeling in front of her. As her eyes became more focused and her head cleared, she concentrated on this strange woman. Her plain simple dress was tied with a leather belt. Dark blond hair was tied back away from her face revealing smooth skin. Her dark green eyes captured Zoe's attention for they were like deep pools of strength and character. She was fearless.

Zoe could not seem to speak for a few minutes, but finally she found her voice. "I'm feeling better, I think." She frantically looked around, "Where are the wolves?"

"Long gone they are—not a thing to fear now."

"Thank you…for helping me."

"Aww, not at all—don't give it another thought." The woman smiled at Zoe—a smile that went all the way to her eyes, which seemed more expressive than words. "Careful you must be in these woods, lass. I just stepped out to snatch some mushrooms to add to my stew or I would not have seen you."

"T'is always meanness that guides Kavian's path. He's the leader of the wolves he is, and he never wearies of doing evil. True this forest is filled with many creatures seeking to harm others—wild boars, bears, panthers, and more. Be sure—t'is not the King's side they are on. Durgalt is their leader. They hunt and kill for him. Oh, pardon my manners, my name's Feena…Feena O'Berry. You'll be staying with me 'til you finish your training. And what would you be called?"

Raising one eyebrow, she replied, "Zoe Newbridge. How did you know I was coming?"

The woman paused and looked puzzled at Zoe, but did not answer her question. "Soon we begin your training. As it is, you are defenseless against these creatures. So tell me, did you meet up with the greulas yet?

"Gruelas?"

"Aye, they are darkness themselves, shadows of what they once were. Evil controls them now so that they no longer even look like they once did. They were once the King's most majestic creatures—eagles. T'is truth they fell to the evil ways of Durgalt and changed to the foul creatures they are now. Thank the King that not all the eagles fell. More awful altogether is that they torment their victims. They are small at first, and you'll not be believing this, but they grow in size the more you listen to them—filtering into your mind and twisting your thoughts."

Zoe thought a moment. "I did see two shadows that swooped down in front and behind me. I was terrified."

"Well, then you saw them. This forest is full of gruelas. They reproduce here and follow everyone that passes through Hemlock Forest. Durgalt has ordered them to pounce upon their prey and whisper murmurings which cause their victims to fear. They know that fear keeps most from walking forward on their chosen path."

"This journey is getting more and more eerie. I wanted adventure but this is too dangerous. Tell me, why do you live in this terrible forest?"

"My purpose is clear, lass; it is two-fold. I live here to bring light to the darkness of the forest. Happy I am to do this. The King also sends people here for me to train. To overcome fear, no better place than this, my dear!"

"What do you mean—what kind of training?"

"The kind of training that will make it possible for you to continue on your journey to Remiah—t'would be a sad day if you did not know how to deal with the gruelas, defend yourself from Durgalt's followers, or how to shoot a bow. Defenseless you are, so I used my bow to give these wolves a good fright."

"But I have never even picked up a bow."

"A young one, you are. You'll have no problem at all. Quick as the animals are, you must learn to be quicker. But who knows, lass? Would it not be wonderful if they came to the King's side to serve Him? But for now t'is time to eat, so let's get you on your feet. We'll go to my cottage. Then, you have much to learn."

He gives us the strength to do
any task that He asks of us.

Part II
Preparing for
the Journey

Chapter Four

He trains my hands for battle, so that my arms
can bend a bow of bronze.
Psalm 18:34

Zoe was relieved to have shelter for the night—just the thought of spending the night alone in Hemlock Forest was terrifying, causing her to shiver. They walked to Feena's garden and picked vegetables for their midday meal, though it was already long past noon. Inside Feena's little cottage, Zoe smelled a delicious aroma. There was a fire going with a pot of boiling broth. Feena quickly cut the vegetables and added them to the steaming mixture.

"Is there anything I can do?" Zoe offered.

"No, no, just rest your wee head. Our meal will be along shortly."

Zoe watched Feena as she cooked. She seemed young, yet somehow Zoe sensed that she was older than she looked because of her wisdom. She was large-boned, strong, and self-assured. Her hair did not have a single strand of gray in it. She was a strange woman, yet intriguing.

Soon Feena placed steaming bowls of soup on the table. While they were eating, Zoe saw a huge bear rug and asked her, "How did you learn to shoot so well?"

"I was nearly lost to that bear. Aye, a friend shot it and saved my life. He taught me how to shoot the bow, he did. Every day I practiced for hours until I finally hit my mark and I still practice daily. Here, have some more bread, lass."

While Zoe ate, she asked a question that she had been wondering about since they met. "May I ask how old you are Feena?"

Feena smiled. "Fifty-eight, I am."

Zoe's eyes widened, "What's your secret?"

"Well," she said slowly, "I serve the King. I believe He keeps me young so I can do all He has asked of me. T'is true I also made the journey to Remiah."

"You did?"

"Aye. Some seven years ago me mother died and life seemed so bleak to me. I never married, you see, and she was everything to me. Soon after she passed, I received an invitation from the King to go to Remiah. I decided to go because I felt I needed to do something significant with me life."

Zoe listened intently. "I knew how to shoot the bow so I could protect myself, but t'was a hard trip. Durgalt was constantly after me. A year it took to finally arrive in Remiah. I learned so much about myself that year—I discovered I wasn't as strong as I thought I was."

"Wait a minute Feena. You're a strong woman!"

"No, I do not mean physically. I thought I could take care of everything, but t'was not so. Durgalt and his many followers attacked me constantly, they did. T'would have been much better if I had turned to the King for help, instead of fighting on me own. When I finally learned to do that, He helped me, and I was able to finish my trip in peace, without striving. I was a proud and arrogant woman then. Now I live for the King and I try to live in His strength."

Feena had a faraway look. "Me mother used to talk about the King too—a kind woman she was."

"May I ask you another question?"

Feena nodded. "What is Remiah like?"

"T'is the most peaceful, beautiful place I have ever seen, and perfect in every way. But what I loved the most was visiting the King there."

Zoe stared at nothing in particular. "It all seems like a dream to me right now...and a distant one at that."

"Oh, do not think that way! Become real it will the closer you get to Remiah. T'would do you well to call on the King for help early, lass." Feena grabbed Zoe's hands. "When I was in Remiah the King told me what He wanted me to do here in Hemlock Forest."

"You mean you were able to talk to Him…just like you and I are talking now?"

"Why of course, girl. How else can you get to know Him?"

"You are right, I suppose. Until I received His invitation to go to Remiah, I just thought it was a story, like a fairy tale."

"Aye, t'is all true. Now, how do you feel after eating?"

Zoe smiled, "Much better, thank you."

"Good lass, because we need to start your training."

When they went outside, Zoe nervously searched for the wolves. Feena saw her distressed look, "You need not be scared for their return will not be soon."

Feena lowered her voice to a whisper. "You may not believe this lass, but an enchanted forest this is. Many animals can talk here."

"They really talk?"

"When I first heard them," Feena laughed, "I thought I'd lost me mind! The good ones as well as the bad ones talk."

Zoe was shocked and she could not speak for almost a minute. Finally she said, "How did they learn to talk?"

"Well, as it happened, the King was visiting Hemlock Forest one day and He gave the gift of speech to all the animals present— even the wolves you saw today. T'is an honorable King we serve because they have used their gift for bad and He never took it back. He is hoping one day that they will turn from their evil ways and follow Him."

"That *is* something! I can't wait to talk to some of your friends!"

"Soon enough lass, but for now, let's walk to the clearing behind me cottage. You have much to learn."

They came to a large open area set up as an archery range. "Try holding this bow. How does it feel?"

Zoe lifted it. "Heavier than I thought it would be!"

"Aye, but you'll be getting used to it. Now first, watch how I hold the bow and the way I'm standing. See, my feet are against this line I marked. Aim I shall for that circle on the tree."

Feena pulled the arrow back, aimed, and let it go. "Bulls-eye!" Zoe was amazed as Feena shot several more times and hit the target dead center every time.

"The best way to get a clear shot is to turn sideways to your target, keeping your feet shoulder width apart. Your head needs to be turned, facing your mark."

Zoe looked stiff and awkward. "Loosen up Zoe or t'will be hard to hit your target.

She relaxed some. "Very good lass. Now hook your first three fingers on the string to get a feel for the bow." As Zoe attempted to do this, she lost her grip and dropped it.

"T'is all right, now try again. Put your arrow on the bow. It needs to stay level with your shoulders. Turn your shooting elbow away from the string. Perfect! Next, draw the string crosswise from your shoulders. Make sure you stand straight."

Zoe dropped her head in frustration. "Feena, you're telling me to do too many things at once!"

"T'would do you well to stay calm, lass. Now back to your shooting. Your string should touch the middle of your chin with your pointing finger under your chin. Now look at your target and aim. T'is very important that your eye never leave your target. If you lose your focus, you've lost your target."

Feena watched as Zoe got into position. "Pull back your shooting arm as far as your ear and then release your arrow."

To Zoe's disappointment, she watched the arrow fly in the air and land twenty feet from the target.

"You'll hit that target lass. T'was right in line with the circle. Now try again."

Practicing for another hour, still struggling, she was able to shoot a little farther each time.

"Zoe, t'is time to quit for now. Proud of you, I am. With all your practicing your arms will surely be sore in the morning."

Zoe did not tell Feena, but she was already hurting. Her upper arms were so tight and sore she could hardly lift them. She felt discouraged, but did not want Feena to know that either.

As they were walking back to the cottage, Feena noticed Zoe looking a little discouraged. "Lass, to believe and have faith, even when things don't seem so good is important. If you believe you can do something—then t'is possible. Keep trying you should. A wonderful surprise it will be when you finish training lass, for then you will be shooting the bow swiftly and accurately."

When they were finally inside, Feena grabbed Zoe and hugged her. "Go lie down a bit while I finish making supper. You need some rest."

Zoe did not argue. She was exhausted from her day. Just as soon as she put her head on the pillow, she fell into a deep sleep. Several hours passed before Feena finally woke Zoe up. She walked sleepily to the table, but became wide-awake when she took the first bite of potato soup. "This is delicious."

"Me mother made this when I was a wee girl."

"Sounds like you had a happy childhood."

"T'was lovely for sure."

"Zoe, tell me about yourself," Feena encouraged.

She fidgeted in her chair. "Well, I'm not so sure you want to hear about my life."

"Well of course I do, lass."

Zoe cleared her throat. "I don't remember my father. He never lived with my mother and me. My mother was beautiful, at least what I can remember of her. She had long brown hair, large blue eyes, and a beautiful smile."

With a far-off look, Zoe continued. "I remember how she would tell me stories every day and sing me to sleep every night. I stayed with some other lady during the day when my mother worked. But when she was home, sometimes we would bake sweet cakes. My time with her was very happy. That is about all I remember of my mother."

Zoe stopped and tears filled her eyes. "I'm sorry Feena. I don't talk about this much."

Feena laid a comforting hand on Zoe's shoulder, making her feel safe to continue. She wiped her eyes, cleared her throat, and began again.

"The last time I saw my mother was when I was four, almost five. I remember we went to visit her sister, my Aunt Agatha, and I played with my cousins that afternoon. Mother stayed a while and then she told me she had to go. She hugged me for a long time before she said goodbye. I remember seeing tears in her eyes. She walked out of my aunt's house and never came back. It hurt like nothing had ever hurt in my whole life—still does when I think about it. I could not believe that she didn't love me anymore. She acted so much like she loved me when we were together. I asked my aunt where she was, but she would never tell me."

Feena reached over to gently stroke her back. "It must have hurt, lass, but I have to believe something good is going to come even from this."

Zoe looked doubtful. "Nothing has yet. I mean no one has heard from her since the day she left.

Zoe seemed to be in deep thought, then spoke again. "My aunt and cousins treated me kindly, but I never really felt part of their family. So when I was fifteen, I asked my aunt if I could work and live in town with Geneva, an older woman who was my friend. She was a seamstress and I loved her dearly. My aunt agreed to let me go."

Zoe's brow furrowed. "I moved in with Geneva and worked for her for two years. She taught me everything about sewing that she knew. At times, she was stern and uncompromising as she trained me. She made me remake almost everything until it was perfect. I hated doing it over and over, but I now know that it is what made me the kind of seamstress I am today."

"And what kind is that?"

Zoe looked down and pretended to pick up a crumb on the floor. "I am in high demand as a seamstress in Brenlough. I make very intricately designed gowns for the ladies in our village."

"Ah, a highly skilled seamstress. Well, it's in you then."

"What's in me?"

"Determination. In your sewing you did your best. So it will be with the bow."

Zoe gave her an unsure look and Feena smiled. "You will see, lass."

Feena walked over to the fire, took the kettle off, and made some tea as Zoe continued her story.

"Geneva was like a mother to me. She was the one who told me stories about the King—but that is all they seemed like at the time—*stories*. Now I'm wondering if she made the journey to Remiah too. When she was dying, she tried to tell me something about Remiah, but never finished. She did say the King was wonderful, very kind to her, and that He taught her how to love. I never understood that since He lived so far away. It all seemed like a happy fairy tale. I have yet to meet the King, and I often wonder if I will ever know for sure whether this is all real. It seemed like some enchanted land that sounded nice—until I had a dream. If that truly was Remiah, then it is the most beautiful place anywhere. You're the first person I know that has actually been there."

Zoe took a sip of tea. "Anyway, I lived with Geneva for those two years. Other than the memories I have with my mother, it was the happiest time of my life. She helped me forget how much I missed my mother."

Feena took Zoe's hands in her own. "Hard it was, Zoe, but I know a whole new life truly awaits you. What happened next?"

"Oh yes. Sadly, Geneva passed away when I was seventeen—just a year ago. She left all she owned to me since I was the closest family she had. A few days before she died, she told me that there was no one else she would rather see have her things. I know she genuinely loved me as the daughter she never had. She also left me her business and all the money she had saved through the years. She was seventy-five when she died, so she had built up quite a savings. Shortly after I received the money, I bought a beautiful piece of land that has a stream. Then I paid some men in the village to build my little stone cottage facing that stream. Within six months I moved out of Geneva's rented business and into my new home. I have been living there ever since. All of Geneva's customers became my customers."

Zoe looked far away. "I still miss her."

Feena smiled. "A really special woman Geneva was. I would have liked her I believe."

Zoe smiled and put her long brown hair behind her ears. "I am sure you would have."

Feena got the teakettle and refilled their cups. "At eighteen you have already accomplished much in your life. Just think, t'will soon be time for you to continue on this grand adventure—one that you will never forget!"

"I am looking forward to that. But I still can't seem to forget the past...I just wish I could have lived with my mother all those years. At times I am still so angry with her. At other times, I miss her so desperately that I wish I could see her again."

Feena hugged her. "Who knows? Maybe someday you will."

"I don't think so. It seems like she would have come to see me before now. I do not even know if she is alive."

"Well, we shall see. But for now, let's get these dishes washed."

After they finished, they talked a while longer. Soon Zoe was yawning. Feena sleepily said, "Bedtime it is. Our day shall be full tomorrow so let's bid each other a good night."

"Sounds fine to me Feena. Thank you again for everything."

"Make no mention of it. I'm glad you're here," she said with a smile.

Zoe fell asleep thinking about Feena. She admired the strength and courage she saw in her, and wondered if she could ever be half as brave. But then Feena did say, "when you believe all things are possible."

Determination, endurance, and patience lead to sure victory.

Chapter Five

*"For I am the LORD your God, who upholds your
right hand, who says to you, 'Do not fear, I will help you.'"*
Isaiah 41:13

The early morning light filtered through the small window as Zoe lay in bed recounting her journey so far—the forest, gruelas, wolves, learning how to shoot a bow, and Feena. She sighed as she thought about the difficulties she had faced. It would be hard enough making the journey to Remiah because of the great distance, but adding to it all of the dangers she had already faced and those she would surely have to face along the way made it seem virtually impossible.

She glanced at the dying coals in the fireplace. What would it take to keep going, to have a fire in her heart for the King so she could push forward and finish this journey?

Feena was still sleeping so Zoe decided it was a good time to make an entry in her journal. She wrote about her adventures, but she wrote much more about the deep yearning inside to find her purpose in life. Finally, she laid her journal aside, got up, and washed her face at the washstand. Feena was now up and busily preparing breakfast. "Yumm…what smells so good?"

"It's a hearty breakfast you'll be needing lass. How do ham and eggs, along with some scones, sound to you?"

"Sounds wonderful." Zoe walked over to the fire and noticed the huge amount of food Feena was preparing. "Are you expecting more people?"

"No, this is just for you and me. We'll be needing our strength today so I'll pack what is left of the ham and scones for later. T'would not be good if we ran out of food."

Zoe's brow furrowed. "I don't understand. Do you mean we're going somewhere?" Zoe shuddered at the thought of going back out there with those nasty wolves in the forest.

"Now, now Zoe. You cannot stay here forever. We wouldn't want that map of yours to go to waste. I'm only here to help you prepare for the rest of your journey."

"Even if I continue on my journey, how could I fight so many of the wolves when I am only one?"

"Lass, your worrying must stop for everything will work out." Zoe did not look convinced. "Have faith. The King Himself called you to make this journey. You can do anything with His help."

"Perhaps if I had as much experience with the King as you have had, I might have more faith."

Feena patted Zoe on the shoulder lovingly. "Experience must begin where you are now, lass."

After eating their breakfast and packing provisions for the day, Feena led Zoe through the woods for several minutes until they came to a clear, open area. She yelled, "Antrum...t'is all right to come out."

Turning, they spotted a huge, brown buck coming out of the thicket. His antlers were enormous. Following him was his mate, a gentle, tan doe with large, brown eyes. As they came closer, they gazed cautiously at Zoe.

"My dear friends, this is Zoe. She is in training with me and I want you to meet her."

Antrum walked up to Zoe. "You are welcome here. Anyone serving the King is a friend of ours." Turning toward his mate, he said, "This is Grace."

She came closer to Zoe. "I am very pleased to meet you," she said in a kind, soft-spoken voice.

Zoe stood with her mouth gaping open. "I do not mean to stare but I've never heard animals speak before!"

Grace smiled and Antrum leaned closer to Zoe. "Sometimes, we cannot believe we can talk in your language either. It is a gift from the King you know."

Zoe smiled. "And what a wonderful gift it is."

Antrum seemed pleased. "It is that. Now, we should tell you about Kavian, the leader of the wolves in this forest. He does not live under the protection of the King, but we do because we are the King's followers. You really have nothing to fear, but if you allow fear to control you, then it will, and then you will be in danger."

Zoe's brow furrowed. "I'm beginning to believe that fear has had more control over my life than I realized. I understand what you're saying—I just wish I knew for sure the King was really able to take care of me."

Antrum turned and glanced at Feena. "Well, I'd say that He's already shown you that."

Zoe smiled at Feena and she smiled her beautiful smile back. "T'is so true, Antrum."

Feena abruptly changed the subject. "Antrum, can you call all of our friends so Zoe can meet them?"

"Gladly," he exclaimed, leaping back into the thicket. In no time at all he came back with badgers, rabbits, skunks, squirrels, chipmunks, many kinds of birds, two beautiful, black panthers, and five huge, brown bears. Zoe gasped when she saw a pure white doe emerge from the woods.

The white deer walked up closely to Zoe. Her eyes had the clearness of a pure stream. "My name is Sabah. I am most pleased to meet you. It would be an honor if I could help you at any time."

Zoe could not take her eyes off of her for she was so beautiful. "Thank you, Sabah."

Zoe felt a little overwhelmed with all the animals crowding around her. One of the black panthers spoke. "We welcome you in the name of the King!" The other animals cheered and Zoe did not know if she had ever seen anything so amazing and wonderful.

The two sleek panthers walked up to Zoe. "My name is Bantry," he said in a deep, thundering voice, "and this is my mate, Rose. When you begin your journey again, just call us and we will be there to help. We know many secrets of the forest."

Feena laid her hand on Bantry's shoulder. "My friend, t'is good to see you! It's been far too long since last we met. You and Rose look well."

"Thanks, Feena, as do you."

"Can we talk a bit about Kavian? Have you battled with him lately?"

Bantry's eyes became intense. "Yes, just two days ago, but it was quite a victory for us. He tried to attack our new cub. We have him safely hidden now where it would be most difficult for Kavian to find him. We cannot stay long because we must get back to him, but we did want to welcome Zoe and talk to you."

Feena bent closer to Antrum and whispered, "We must be careful now. He is after Zoe and we must protect her."

Antrum nodded. "You can count on us."

Zoe was talking to Grace when a magnificent eagle landed right in front of them. She was surprised by his great size, having never seen one so close before. His eyes were keen and piercing. "My name is Evan—welcome to our forest." He spoke in a distinctly deep and clear voice.

Before Zoe could respond to Evan, suddenly they heard something move behind them in the bushes. Feena motioned for everyone to be silent. "Bantry, take a look around." She turned to a squirrel, "Fern, check out the trees quickly. Evan, fly high above and report what you see."

As if to hide under her protection, Zoe nervously inched closer to Feena. "Do you think it's Kavian again?"

"That I do not know, but we must be certain he is not following us." They waited in silence until the animals returned. Bantry and Fern found no sign of spies, but Evan had a different report. He had seen a lone wolf enter a cave about two hundred feet from where they were.

Feena said, "We must be on the alert then. He's very likely an enemy spy so we must speak quietly. T'would be best for everyone to be posted during our shooting practice. This signal you must remember, so come quickly when I call." Feena let out a shriek. She sounded like an animal in desperate need.

"Zoe needs much practice, so we must get to work. T'is true friends you are to help."

Bantry whispered, "Feena, we will not be far away so we can hear your signal. Don't worry about anything for we will be here in no time at all."

Everyone said their goodbyes and then the animals quickly departed back into the forest.

"Zoe, we need to climb that hill, set up camp, and begin target practice. We'll be staying the night, we will. T'is those fears of yours that are a problem. Where your fears are strongest is where you must face them."

"I was hoping we could practice and go back to your cottage."

"Not tonight my dear."

Zoe looked doubtful as to the wisdom of Feena's plan, but she did not say anything else about it. Finally, they made it to the top of the hill. "Look around, lass. The thicket below, do you see?" Zoe nodded. "Beyond that you can see my cottage. On the other side of the hill, a path to the right leads between those huge rocks. Do you see it, lass?"

"Yes I do."

"The same path it is that leads to the King's house. We'll set up camp here."

Feena placed the target on a tree about fifty feet from where Zoe stood. She walked back to Zoe and said, "Do you remember how to hold the bow?"

Zoe picked it up, but felt all the soreness from yesterday. Even with the pain, she focused, stood in the proper stance, concentrated on the target, pulling her arm back as far as she could, releasing the arrow.

"Two feet from the target!" Zoe smiled and felt encouraged, so she tried again. Each time she shot the arrow, it inched its way closer. Finally, after shooting for a couple of hours, she hit the target. Zoe ran to see how close she was to the bull's eye—only about three inches away.

"Feena, come look!"

"T'is a grand sight! I knew you could do it."

Zoe grinned and said, "Thank you for helping me."

"Hidden talents lie within you. Dig them out and use them, my girl! Now come, vegetable stew is simmering over the fire. Let's eat and then rest before we get back to work."

"Sounds good, Feena. I'm famished!" They sat down by the campfire and enjoyed a relaxing meal. Zoe glanced over at Feena. She was kind and full of wisdom. She loved the King more than anyone she knew, and she really lived what she believed. Zoe felt like there was much to learn from this wise woman and hoped to stay with her for a long time.

Lying on the mat, she was sleeping more peacefully than she had in a long time. But then she felt Feena urgently tugging on her arm. "Quick, Zoe! Kavian and his pack are in the bushes."

Zoe stood up abruptly. Feena had already grabbed her bow and arrows, so Zoe did the same. "Where are they? I don't see them."

Zoe turned when she heard a growl. Kavian said in a deep, hoarse voice, "Why Feena, how good to see you." Sneering, he continued, "We are not here to see you though. We want the girl."

Feena walked right up to him. "Well, you can forget it. You'll not be getting this one. Go on back to the woods, Kavian, where you belong."

"No one will get hurt *if* you give me the girl. Now move aside Feena!" He bared his teeth and inched closer. Zoe was trembling and felt lightheaded.

Feena stood her ground. "One step further, Kavian, and I'll shoot!"

He grinned, "There are only two of you." Then he called for his clan. "There are twenty of us. You're outnumbered!"

"You leave me no choice." Feena whistled her signal and soon fifty of her friends emerged from the bushes.

Bantry walked up to Kavian and growled. "Leave now. This is not your territory!"

Kavian looked at all the animals ready for battle and realized that they could not defeat so many. "All right," he grimaced. "You may have won this time, but don't think this is the last time you will see me. I have orders to get that girl—and get her I will!"

Kavian and his pack ran back into the woods. Zoe sat down on a nearby rock and put her head in her hands, pondering this mess she was in. *I am endangering the lives of too many just so I can go to Remiah.*

Bantry walked up to her. "Zoe, do not worry about him. He was not very smart to tell us his plan, though we already suspected it. We'll see that you remain safe in the forest at all times. I don't think he will be back for a while anyway."

Zoe raised her head and faced all her new friends. "I know all of you want to help me, and I do appreciate it, but your lives are in danger because of me. Perhaps it would just be best if I went home."

Feena sat down beside her, "Lass, we are helping you because that is what we want to do—what we are called to do. To Remiah the King wants you to go. Remember what I told you—rise above what you are feeling and ask for strength from the King."

Antrum could see the concern in Zoe's eyes. "Don't worry about us. We are under the King's protection and you are too—remember that Zoe. You have to stop doubting and start believing that you can make it to Remiah, all right?"

"I will try—I mean I will."

Antrum was pleased. "Good."

Zoe looked up at everyone. "I really appreciate your help. I have never had such true friends." They all smiled, told Zoe she was welcome, and that they were honored to help.

Feena got everyone's attention. "Bantry, this is the plan. Set up guards around the camp at all times. Through tomorrow we'll be staying, and then head back to my house we will."

"Do not worry—nothing is going to happen to Zoe. We will see to that," Bantry replied.

"True friends you are. Kavian means business this time and she's going to have to be well trained for it. So we better get back to practice."

"Call if you need us, Feena. We will see you soon." They said goodbye and their friends left the clearing.

"Lass t'is time to practice a bit more and then we'll be about finding food in the forest."

After Zoe practiced until her arms could take no more, Feena showed her which mushrooms, berries, and nuts were good to eat, and those that were not. She even showed her some grass that was edible.

They walked back to camp, made a small campfire, and heated up the leftover stew. As they ate, Zoe kept watchful eyes all around her.

Zoe looked down. "I'm really tired, but how can I possibly sleep knowing Kavian and his group are lurking about in the shadows? And remember the gruelas—they like darkness."

"Never fear those in darkness because they fear the light that is growing within you. As long as you are living in peace and do not give into fear, they will not torment you. Bantry and his friends are posted all around us. Evan will guard us as he flies over the whole area. He has the keenest eyesight of anyone I know. Sleep well tonight you should."

Zoe looked doubtful. Feena quickly fell asleep while Zoe gazed up at the stars. She saw a shadow pass over her. Startled, she sat up and looked around and saw another shadow. *Oh, no, the gruelas!* She inched closer to tell Feena about them, but she decided against it. She would not submit to the fear that the gruelas tried to instill. She saw another one pass right next to her. She cringed and closed her eyes. She was so close to Feena now that she could hear her breathing. Then she saw Evan sweep above her.

He called down, "They will trouble you no longer. I will keep watch. But Zoe, you must remember they only grow in strength when you give in to their fearful lies. Ignore them and they will go away. Sleep in peace."

Zoe gratefully shouted, "Thank you so much Evan."

Feena tossed in her sleep, "Lass, did you say something?"

"Just talking to a friend."

Feena turned over and fell back into a deep sleep.

Oh, to live in that kind of peace would be wonderful, thought Zoe as she watched Feena sleep. Zoe tossed and turned for a while, but finally gave in to sleep when she could no longer hold her eyes open. But as she was falling asleep, her last thought was that she must overcome the fears that tormented her. Unbeknownst to Zoe, tomorrow she would face one of the greatest of those very fears.

Anxiety produces fear—trusting Him produces peace.

Chapter Six

And the peace of God, which surpasses all comprehension,
shall guard your hearts and your minds in Christ Jesus.
Philippians 4:7

"Zoe, I have an urgent message for you from Bantry," the little brown rabbit glanced around nervously. "He overheard Kavian talking to the other wolves last night. He plans to attack sometime today. But Bantry also told me to tell you not to worry because we will protect you."

"How does Kavian know we will even be here?"

"He will follow you. He plans to attack wherever you go in the forest."

"I will tell Feena right away. By the way, what is your name?"

"Millie."

"Thank you, Millie."

She stood up on her hind feet, and leaned in to get a little closer to Zoe. "They are watching you from a distance, so be very careful."

"I will." After Millie left, an eerie feeling come over Zoe. She ran to Feena and shared the news.

"Well then, we'd better practice."

"What? I thought when you heard this that we would go back to the cottage."

"Oh no, Zoe. Remember what I told you—there will be no running."

"But what is the point of facing a fear when we could be safe in your cottage?"

Feena sighed. "A long time I have lived in the forest, yet I do not live in fear. Sooner or later you will have to face Kavian."

"Feena, I do not want to face him!"

"You follow the King, so He will give you the strength to do this, lass. Enough said. I need to cook breakfast now."

Breakfast had no taste to Zoe. She picked at her food and ate silently. They cleaned up quickly and began a long day of practicing. Zoe could not fully concentrate because she kept looking around for Kavian. Although this heaviness hung over Zoe, somehow she managed to feel better as the day progressed.

"Good shot, Zoe. Bulls-eye again! Soon enough you will be hitting the bulls-eye more than missing it, lass. Natural as breathing it will be."

While they were talking, the sky began to darken with threatening clouds. As Zoe was looking at the sky she heard something rustle in the leaves, and she whirled around. Her eyes nervously searched the shrubs expecting to see Kavian, but to her relief she saw Bantry instead.

"Oh, I am so glad it's you Bantry!"

"I didn't mean to scare you, but I need to talk to you and Feena about Kavian. I have some more news. Evan spotted him very close to here. Quite frankly, I am surprised he has not already attacked because he has been in the area all day."

Feena moved closer to Bantry. "For sure his purpose is to make us nervous. But we're ready for him, we are. Just wait for my signal before we attack. Perhaps even then we can avoid a battle altogether."

Lightning flashed from the sky, hitting a tree nearby. Feena turned to Zoe, "Stay close to me for there is nothing to worry about. Remember to trust the King!"

Zoe could do nothing but stare at Feena. *How do I trust the King when I have never even seen or spoken to Him?*

To Zoe's utter despair, Kavian appeared just at that moment with about fifty hideous animals. She looked closely at all of them. There were three enormous brown bears, five bobcats, about twenty wolves, and the rest were smaller animals—badgers, squirrels, and skunks.

"I'm here to get the girl. We'll do her no harm if you give her to us now. I'm only taking her back to her house."

"No, Kavian. Go back with you, she will not," Feena said as she signaled her friends to come.

Kavian watched Feena's friends gather, but seemed unconcerned, feeling that he had his best fighters with him. "We can take them easily. This is your last chance, Feena. Give her up to me!"

"No, here she will stay!" Feena raised her bow and told Zoe to do the same. They both aimed at Kavian.

"You will not really use that bow," he smirked. "You don't like hurting others."

Feena said, "Right you are. Others I do not like to hurt, but use it I will! And you know what a good shot I am."

He inched closer to Zoe. Feena yelled, "Get back!"

Not taking her eyes off Kavian, Feena leaned in and whispered to Zoe, "Get ready to shoot."

He backed up and glared at Zoe, "What do you think you're doing?"

Trembling, Zoe took a step forward, "I...I am not going with you, now or ever!"

Kavian again advanced toward Zoe, calling the rest of his group to follow. At the same time, Bantry and his group started walking toward Kavian. Bantry held his gaze steadily on Kavian, but waited for the signal from Feena to attack.

Zoe concentrated her aim on Kavian. *Feena trusts the King...I must trust Him!* Kavian and his followers were getting closer. Suddenly, as Zoe was just about to release her arrow, a huge bolt of lightning flashed, hitting a tree right behind Kavian. He saw it falling but could not quite escape. His leg became trapped under the tree as it crashed to the ground with a vibration that matched the thunder. The rest of his group scattered in panic. Kavian was moaning in pain, but using every ounce of strength within him, he pulled his mutilated leg free, and limped away growling, "I'm not giving up. I will be back..."

They watched as he limped away. Feena looked at Zoe with knowing eyes and said, "Do you now see what I was trying to tell you?"

Zoe nodded her head. "When Kavian was coming closer, I knew I had to trust the King, and then this amazing peace began to flow through my whole body. The tree fell, right when Kavian was about to attack. The King really did take care of me."

Feena smiled that beautiful smile of hers. "That He did!"

Zoe glanced over at the tree that had fallen and saw something sparkling. She walked over to it and saw that it was a key. She picked it up and looked at it closely. *Why it's pure gold, and so heavy,* she mused. "Look Feena, the inscription says **PEACE**. I wonder where this came from?"

Zoe realized that the key was next to the spot that the bolt of lightning had hit. Feena sat down on the fallen tree beside Zoe and hugged her. "Proud of you, I am, Zoe. The King has given you the **Key to PEACE**. It will become part of you now. This key means you have taken the first step to trusting Him. You have learned to receive peace from Him in a tough situation. Keep this key always and hold it dear to your heart. A special gift from the King it is, lass."

As Zoe held the key, she suddenly realized the purpose for the pocket inside of her dress. She placed the key there and felt peace soothingly melt into her heart. She savored the moment and smiled—for it felt like a treasure had been deposited deep within her.

Feena smiled. "On this journey, you will learn so much more. This is just the beginning."

Quietly, all the animals gathered around Zoe and Feena. Bantry said, "Would you like for us to go back with you to your cottage now?"

Zoe answered, "Yes, if it is all right with Feena, I would like that." Feena nodded her approval. "Thank you for everything."

Bantry bowed and said, "My pleasure."

A torrential rain began falling so they packed quickly and headed back. The animals said goodbye once they reached Feena's cottage and silently disappeared into the forest. Zoe and Feena thankfully entered the homey cottage and started a blazing fire. They both sat down and warmed their feet.

As Zoe gazed at the fire, she thought about everything that had happened today. It had to be the King who sent the lightning to fell that tree. He really did protect her. She wanted to always live in the kind of peace she felt today. She took the key out of her pocket and held it in her hand. She realized that fear really did not have to control her any longer—gruelas or Kavian did not matter. She knew with all her heart that the King was real and she would not doubt again.

Zoe took her journal out and quickly wiped a tear so it would not fall and wet the pages. She wrote about the new peace she had received. When she finished, she felt warm, calm, peaceful, and full of gratitude toward the King. The burden of fear she had carried for so long was gone. She had given it to the King, who gladly took it and in return gave her His peace.

The key to peace is to trust and rest
in Him with all things.

Chapter Seven

"Only fear the L ORD and serve Him in truth with all your heart; for consider what great things He has done for you."
I Samuel 12:24

Zoe was thankful for the reprieve from Kavian in the weeks that followed. She made good use of the time by continuing to practice her archery skills, and talking more to Feena about the King. Zoe would never forget the day she asked Him into her life.

"Feena, I believe the King is real—not just a fantasy any longer. I want to know Him like you do."

"To know the King lass, t'is important to spend time with Him. This is how I know the King so well."

"What do you mean? Does He come here to talk with you?"

"Well, no—not very often, but I do talk to Him, just like I talk to you. T'is wonderful how He shows me He is listening in His own special way. T'will never be a better time to tell Him you believe He is real and that you want Him to be King of your life forever."

"Thank you, Feena. I think I will go and do just that." Zoe told the King all that was on her heart, that she did believe in Him, and that she wanted to follow Him forever. He replied with a cleansing that came over her like a bath—not on the outside but on the inside. Then the peace, which had so recently been given to her by the King, flowed even deeper within her. Her heart was His forever now.

She found Feena and talked to her about trusting the King more deeply and how to let go of her fears. Zoe was changing, but she could not know how much she had changed until she faced that fear again.

"Feena, I'm going outside to practice."

"T'is a good idea. I will be out in a little while." As Zoe went outside, Feena watched and suddenly began feeling apprehensive. Perhaps she should go with her, but as she prayed to the King, He told her that this would be a test that Zoe needed to face alone. However, she knew she could pray for her, and that she did.

Zoe straightened the target on the tree and walked about sixty feet from it. She practiced for a while, then decided to rest for a few minutes. As she sat down, she saw something move by a tree near her target. She watched closely for a few minutes, seeing nothing, she stood up and continued to practice.

Feena was watching Zoe from her window, and she saw what was moving in the bushes—Kavian. As far as she could tell, there was no one else with him. She watched to see if he would make his move. She began praying to the King to give Zoe strength.

Just as Zoe shot her arrow, Kavian came out of the bushes, yelling, "Good shot!"

Zoe gasped. In his usual loud and gravelly voice, he said, "Wouldn't you like to show your friends back home how well you can shoot now?"

Zoe wondered why he was being so nice. She could not find words to answer him.

"Oh come on, you can talk to me. I mean you no harm. I can safely take you back home and you will not have to be afraid anymore. You do miss your home don't you?"

Zoe still did not speak—all she could do was stare at him. Although his leg was still injured, and he was obviously still in pain, Kavian stubbornly dragged it and kept limping closer.

"You cannot stay here forever, Zoe. Feena will be leaving soon. She always leaves this time of year to go camping in the mountains. Then what will you do? You will be here all alone."

Feena was listening the whole time. Kavian was lying! She never left home other than to check on her friends in the woods, and then not for very long. Feena felt certain that Kavian had no intention of taking her back home—he was going to kill her.

"She will probably be leaving in the next few days. I heard Antrum talking about it. So what are you going to do? Stay here alone or let me take you back home where it's safe."

Zoe could not understand why Feena had not mentioned that she was leaving. All Zoe could do was pray to the King for His guidance. Finally she was able to talk. "I...I cannot go with you."

Kavian was still inching closer. "Why? I told you I would not hurt you."

Zoe stood firm. "I'm not going with you!"

Kavian was beginning to get impatient. "Then you are choosing to stay here alone, without the protection of Feena."

Feena was still listening and watching from the cottage. She could see that Kavian was not going to try and convince her to go with him very much longer—he just did not have that kind of patience. She started to pick up her bow and arrow just in case Zoe needed her. But no, she had specific instructions from the King to let Zoe handle this alone. All she could do was pray.

"I am a follower of the King...He will protect me!"

That made Kavian angry. He began snarling, baring his teeth, and pacing back and forth. He was less than thirty feet away when he started running toward her. She knew he was going to attack, so she quickly took her last arrow, placed it in the bow, aimed, and shot.

It was a perfect shot. She aimed for his shoulder and hit him squarely. The arrow penetrated deep into his muscle, leaving Kavian motionless. Zoe slowly inched closer to examine him. To her relief, he was still breathing, but blood pooled around his shoulder and he appeared unconscious.

A single tear fell down Zoe's cheek, not only because she felt so guilty about shooting him, but because she had never hurt an animal in her entire life. Feena ran out of the cottage when she saw Kavian on the ground. She hugged Zoe and comforted her.

"T'was the right thing you did Zoe. Taking you back to your home, he was not going to do."

Zoe just stared at Feena. "You were listening to our conversation, and you didn't come to help me?"

"I couldn't, lass. Alone you needed to face this battle. T'was time to see if you would pass or fail what the King has been teaching you. For sure I was praying for you though. Do you realize what you have done?"

Zoe looked puzzled. "I shot Kavian."

"T'is true lass. But more importantly you faced your fear and you overcame it! Fear did not control you. You had control over fear."

Zoe realized it was true. "I just knew the King was with me."

"T'is true when you have peace in your life, you can face any situation calmly, without fear."

Zoe and Feena turned when they heard rustling in the leaves and saw wolves by the bushes. Feena yelled to them, "Come and get Kavian, and away with you all!"

Using their teeth to get a hold of the scruff of his neck, the wolves managed to pull him away. *Will he live?* Zoe wondered.

Feena interrupted her thoughts and said: "Lass, I know you didn't want to shoot him, but he chose this. T'is never easy to hurt another creature, but sometimes you must. Now let's go inside. Your day was hard, but you handled it well. Proud of you I am!"

Even though it was near suppertime, Zoe fell asleep and did not wake up until the next morning. No nightmares awakened her as they sometimes did, for she was filled with the King's peace.

Living in His peace consumes and overpowers the enemy's fear—every time.

Part III
The
Journey Begins

Chapter Eight

And I will betroth you to Me in faithfulness.
Then you will know the LORD.
Hosea 2:20

Zoe continued to sharpen her shooting skills daily. Now she rarely missed her mark so Feena felt confident that she had developed the skills necessary to survive. Zoe was also learning to overcome her fears and she was gaining more confidence each day. Since her last encounter with Kavian, Zoe had developed an even deeper trust in the King. As much as she would miss her, Feena now knew the time had come for Zoe to leave.

They were both outside practicing when Feena approached Zoe. "Lass, how do you feel about your shooting skills?"

Zoe thought a moment. "It was definitely a challenge at first, but I feel fairly confident in my ability now, and it is all due to your excellent training. Thank you, Feena."

Feena grabbed Zoe by the shoulders and looked her straight in the eyes. "T'was you who had the talent—I just helped you find it. Proud of you I am!"

Feena cleared her throat. "Zoe, I know this may be hard for you to hear, but t'is time for you to continue on your journey."

Zoe looked puzzled. "I don't think I'm ready to leave. What I mean is that I have so much more to learn from you."

"You have learned everything I was supposed to teach you. Change is always hard Zoe, but t'is time for the next part of your adventure."

Zoe felt tears filling her eyes. "It's going to be so difficult to leave you Feena—I'll miss you so much!" She impulsively grabbed Feena and hugged her tightly.

"I feel the same Zoe and I will miss you too, but we will see each other again, and soon I venture to say. Remiah is where you want to go, is it not, lass?"

"Yes I do, but come with me Feena! Then we could be together and you could teach me even more. I admire your wisdom and want to be just like you."

"What a lovely thing to say and I thank you for it, but wisdom is something you learn from experience. When you learn from your mistakes and don't repeat them, that is true wisdom. Oh it was a grand adventure to Remiah, but this is where I must stay so I can train others, lass. But you will not be making the journey alone." She pointed to the porch. "A gift for you I have."

Zoe turned around and saw a young wolf with striking blue eyes. Shocked, she said, "This is your gift to me?"

"All wolves are not like Kavian and the rest of his ruffians. Plenty of wolves are on the King's side too. The pup's mother is Reesa, but I don't know who his father is. Reesa can talk but this wee one has not yet spoken. He is six months old, so he still has a bit more growing to do, but a fine friend and protector he will be on your journey."

Zoe called the wolf and he came. She bent down and looked at his gentle eyes and then scratched him behind the ears. "Thank you Feena. I believe he will."

Feena watched as Zoe played with the pup a few minutes. "What will you name him?"

"I don't know yet. I think I shall get to know him first and then see what name fits him best."

"'Grand idea! Come on, lass, let's sit on the steps a few minutes and talk." Feena threw a stick to the pup and he caught it. Zoe smiled but turned her attention to Feena when she grabbed her hand.

"You'll do just fine on your journey to Remiah. Trust the King, for no matter what comes your way. He will always protect you my dear."

Zoe thought about Feena. "You have taught me so much—how to shoot a bow and arrow, fight my fears, and trust the King. The kindness you have shown to all the animals is so amazing, and you are even kind to Kavian!"

"Is he not something? Strange, but sometimes I feel sorry for him. T'is loneliness I have seen in his eyes. Hard to believe this because of the way he acts, but he needs a friend too. I wonder…oh well, never mind."

"No, what do you wonder?"

"Well…maybe if someone would treat him kindly, perhaps he would change. T'is what I have thought for a while now. Maybe he would turn to our side if someone would be even a wee bit nice to him."

Zoe was amazed at this thought. "That would be a miracle! It is hard to imagine someone that mean could ever change."

"For something like this to happen, we must have faith. T'is time to go to bed now though. You need a good night's rest to start your grand adventure!" They went inside and drank some warm milk and then settled in for the night.

Zoe went to her bed and the wolf followed her. He already seemed to know that he and Zoe were going to be together from now on. "You know what fella? I'm going to name you Brogan. How do you like it?" He wagged his tail. Zoe snuggled under the thick woolen blankets realizing that this was the last night she would be sleeping in this warm bed. Brogan hopped up on the foot of the bed, and turned around several times until he found a comfortable position. They both fell into a deep and peaceful sleep.

⋆─▭ ✳ ▭─⋆

Sunlight was filtering through the window when they awoke. Feena had started making breakfast for them. "Sit down, Zoe. Breakfast is almost ready. How'd you sleep?"

Groggily, Zoe replied, "Very peacefully—how about you?"

"Oh fine," Feena said hesitantly. "My mind held many thoughts last night, mostly about you."

A tear slid down Zoe's cheek. "I'm going to miss you, Feena."

Feena tried to hold back the tears, but her eyes were soon watery too. "You must make this journey, Zoe, and you can be certain that I will be praying for you."

They ate a quiet breakfast while they looked at Zoe's map. Feena told her everything she knew about the upcoming landmarks and cautioned her to stay on the path just as the King had told her, for certain areas were full of the enemy's followers.

"According to the map, your next destination is the Cliffs of Fenner. Beyond the cliffs is another forest called Runden Forest. T'is right here on the map. Lass, you must be very careful to stay on the path because there are many evil creatures lurking about in that forest. The King's territory it was—until Durgalt turned to the evil side long ago and took it over." With a twinkle in her eye, she continued, "But there is one part of the forest that still belongs to some friends of mine, the elves. T'is true one day we're going to take the whole forest back for the King."

Zoe's eyes widened in astonishment. "Elves? You mean there are really elves who live in that forest?"

Feena grinned, "Why of course, lass. You will meet them—of this I am sure. Arden is their leader while his father is away. A fine young man he is. He is just, honest, and has tremendous respect among all who know him."

Zoe had a far off look. "I cannot wait to meet the elves. I have always thought they were just fairy tale creatures."

"Oh, call them fairy tale creatures I would not, and some are part human you know. They just have special gifts that make them different."

"Really? What kinds of gifts?"

"Our King has given them a special gift of prophecy."

"You mean telling the future?"

"Yes, serve the King for generations they have. T'is wonderful how faithful they are to follow Him. For this He gave them the gift of prophecy. He knew they would use it wisely, only to further the

King's cause. Keen eyesight and hearing are special gifts they have too. Rarely can anyone surprise them because they can hear and see better than most animals. And they are also skilled at shooting the bow."

"Well, you and I can do that."

"But not with their distance and accuracy."

"Also, King Ronan, the leader of the elves in Runden Forest has a special gift of healing."

Zoe was so amazed, finding the elves to be even more intriguing. "Now I'm really anxious to meet them all!"

"Before I forget, I'll contact Evan so he can tell Arden, King Ronan's son, that you are coming through Runden Forest. They can be of great help to you. But the Cliffs of Fenner will be your first destination and you must be very careful Zoe."

"I think I will be fine. When I was a little girl there were cliffs near my aunt's cottage, and I used to climb them almost every day. But I am thankful you gave me Brogan—I will feel better having him along."

"T'is a fine name, Brogan—fits him well it does."

They talked for a while longer and before long it was time for Zoe to leave. Feena packed enough food to last for a week, as well as a blanket, candles, a warm cape, cloth for bandaging, and a new pair of boots.

Full of gratitude, Zoe hugged Feena. "Thanks so much…for everything. I will…never forget you!"

Feena's eyes were shining with tears. "Fine you will be, lass. The greatest adventure of your life you are about to enjoy, Zoe!"

Zoe walked out of the cottage and turned around savoring the last glimpses of Feena. She waved goodbye and then marched resolutely back to her chosen path with Brogan at her side.

⤙⚹⤚

For hours they walked with Zoe's thoughts still on Feena. She was going to miss her and would never forget the time she had with her. She was truly a wonderful woman, really the nicest person she had ever known. She was still feeling a bit sad when she noticed the path began to change from sandy and smooth to a rock-strewn road. At first the rocks were small, but the farther they went, the bigger and more jagged they became.

"I cannot understand where all these rocks are coming from Brogan," she said as they crept along the road. It was slow, but they were making steady progress. Suddenly, Brogan began barking at something. Zoe looked down and saw a large copper-colored snake right at her feet!

She tried to move away, but before she could the snake leaped forward at her! Brogan grabbed the snake with his mouth just as it was about to sink its teeth. He kept snapping it back and forth until it went limp. When he put the dead snake down, Zoe saw that it was poisonous by the shape of its head.

"Brogan, you just saved my life!" The large puppy came and sat down next to Zoe, and she hugged him until her trembling stopped.

"Thank you Brogan. I don't know what I would have done without you." She realized that just as Feena had said, he had become a dear friend and protector.

When she finally felt calm enough to continue, they started the journey again. As they walked along the rocky road, the rocks felt like knives to their feet. Zoe looked at the soles of her boots and saw holes in them. Then she noticed something very strange. Next to the road on which they were walking was a smooth, sandy road with no rocks. She looked on her map and could not find that road on it. Maybe she should change roads. It ran parallel to this one and it was going in the same direction. But then she remembered she had strict instructions not to leave the path under any circumstances.

Walking became more and more difficult. Brogan heard something and quickly turned around. He began growling. Zoe watched as a couple who looked to be in their fifties approached them. They seemed to be in a great deal of pain and they were breathing very hard. Zoe asked them if they were okay.

"No, we are not! Just look at our feet! I cannot believe we have to follow this road, when the one next to us is nice and smooth. We are changing roads. Come on Emma. Do you and your...you have a wolf as a pet?" Brogan growled at the man, and he backed away.

Not liking their comment, Zoe replied shortly, "Yes, I do."

"Good watchdog? How about coming with us?"

"No, we're going to stay on this road." Zoe thought she at least needed to be hospitable to these strange people. "Would you like some water?"

"No thanks." They looked at the wolf. "Did you know he is injured? Look at his feet—they're bleeding! If you'd walk on the smooth road over there, it would give him time to heal. Come on, what do you say?"

Zoe looked longingly over at the road. "I wish we could, but no, we cannot. We have to go now, but we wish you well on your journey."

"Suit yourself, but obviously you don't care for your wolf or you would give him a break from this awful road. He's not even full grown from the looks of him." They gave Zoe a look that sent chills up her spine. Shaking their heads at her, they walked over to the sandy road and continued walking.

Zoe stood for a moment and watched them leave. She was feeling quite guilty about Brogan. She looked down at him, "Your feet *are* bleeding! I'm so sorry Brogan." She sat down beside him. "I wish I could help you...but what can I do?"

She looked around at their surroundings. "It's getting dark so we'll need to find some shelter soon, then we can rest. Everything will be fine, Brogan."

Zoe began looking for shelter—any shelter. She and Brogan continued to walk in pain, but there was no choice. They had to keep going. Then a man approached them. She recognized him, but from where?

His light blue eyes lit up with kindness. "Hello, Zoe! You have a new friend I see."

Gratefully, she saw it was Kieran, the messenger who had delivered her invitation to Remiah from the King! With relief, she smiled. "Yes, his name is Brogan."

The messenger bent down to pat Brogan. "The King has sent me to show you shelter for the night."

They left the road and he led them to a cave behind some brush. They had to duck their heads to go inside, but it was warm and dry. She looked around. "This cave is not on my map, is it?"

"Yes, it is. Look closely." Zoe took out the map and did see that the cave was on it. She would have walked right by it.

"I have brought you some healing balm. Come, sit down." Zoe looked at the cream closely. It looked like jelly, but it was clear. When he opened the jar a wonderful lavender smell filled the air. The messenger spread it on Brogan and then Zoe's feet, and to her amazement, they were both healed instantly. The wounds shriveled up and were replaced by clear new skin. "Keep this with you. You may need it in the future, but remember to use it only when absolutely necessary."

The messenger continued. "In your walk, you will find that another path may seem right, and may even look inviting, but be careful and allow only the King to guide you. The enemy can make many roads look inviting. He will tempt you with these paths especially when you are weak, so do not be deceived. Remember the goal you have set, and most of all, remember the King's instructions. You must work every day toward achieving this goal, for it will lead to the fulfillment of your destiny. Keep walking forward, and stay close to Him so you will remain on the path that has been especially selected for you.

"The enemy will use any possible way to keep you from what you were born to accomplish. When the enemy throws guilt at people, most do not know how to handle it. Guilt is never sent from the King—He will draw hearts to repentance, but never does He condemn. He brings peace and healing.

"It is sad that the couple left their chosen path. Before they saw you, they had already determined in their hearts that they were going to find an easier road. Because they were not following the King's will for their lives, they were wide open to an attack from the enemy. Since they were determined to leave their path, the enemy began using them to try and persuade you to leave your road as well and they didn't even realize it. Unless they repent, they will wander farther and farther from the King in their walk. This is an important lesson, for you must seek the King constantly for guidance to remain in His will.

"Sadly, the couple does not know that the path they are on will turn into a dead-end road. That smooth path will take them many miles away from their destined path and they will lose much time in their journey, but the King will even then give them an opportunity to turn around and follow the path that He has chosen for them. You have been faithful to stay on the road the King has selected for you, and as a reward you are given this key." He then handed Zoe a gold key with the inscription of *FAITHFULNESS.* Zoe immediately placed the key in her pocket and realized that she would never leave the King.

"Thank you for delivering this key to me. I know we stayed on the right path, but this key seemed fairly easy to receive. Why was this?"

"The King has seen the devotion and faithfulness in your heart for Him. It was confirmed when you stayed on your chosen path—the seemingly more difficult path of the two choices you faced. You have determination to follow the King, which will be the foundation for faithfulness to grow in your heart. He is pleased with you, Zoe. As a reward this key was given to you.

The messenger stood and walked to the opening of the cave. "The King has sent you a gift, a basketful of provisions for you to enjoy. I must leave now, but remember He is always with you—even when you cannot feel Him with you. Blessings in the name of the King."

Zoe curtsied. "Thank you…for everything."

Kieran smiled, turned, and walked through the narrow opening of the cave into the falling shadows of the sun. After he left, Zoe opened the basket and found cheese, bread, fruit, nuts, and wafers. She decided to save the food Feena had given them for another time, for it would keep. They ate almost everything except for some wafers and cheese. They drank from the water the King had provided, which never seemed to run dry. The more they drank, the more their strength was renewed.

Brogan was so energized from being healed and full that he found a stick on the ground and brought it to Zoe to throw. They played the stick game until Brogan finally tired out, plopped down on the ground, and went fast to sleep.

Zoe took out her journal and wrote all that she had learned about faithfulness. She now realized that to be faithful she would follow the King—no matter what.

The key to faithfulness is being fully devoted while drawing closer to Him—never leaving the path of your destiny.

Chapter Nine

"Be strong and courageous, do not be afraid...for the
Lord your God is the one who goes with you.
He will never fail you or forsake you."
Deuteronomy 31:6

The Cliffs of Fenner appeared to be a small landmark on the map. *Good,* Zoe thought, *perhaps they will be small cliffs.* She put the map down and examined her old boots. She slipped them off and stuck her finger through the right toe. Laying them aside, she thankfully put on the new leather boots that Feena had given her.

"Come on Brogan, we need to go." He came quickly when she called. And thus they began the next phase of their journey.

As they walked onto the path again, the rocks slowly disappeared and the road became smooth and wide. They pleasantly passed several miles of yellow and purple wildflowers that gently swayed in the wind. But as the cliffs came into view, her eyes widened with horror. From a distance they looked insurmountable. How was she going to climb them? Her fears were realized as she approached the cliffs. There did not appear to be any way to hold on to anything. Climbing would mean sure and certain death if they fell. Then as she studied them for a long time, to her delight she noticed a very narrow opening that appeared to be a path leading straight up and through.

"Well Brogan. I think we can climb these cliffs after all." Brogan's ears went up and he wagged his tail as if to encourage her. "We might as well get started."

As they climbed, the incline became so steep at times that she was forced to crawl, inching her way to the top. She slid down the cliff several times scraping and bruising her legs in the process. Brogan followed carefully behind her, but he also struggled on the dusty path. This was proving far more difficult than Zoe had anticipated. All day they struggled, finally making it to the top of the first level. They sat down to rest on the small landing. It was mid-afternoon, and as Zoe looked up, she saw that there were at least two more levels to climb. Many thoughts came to her mind but predominantly, *How are we ever going to make it to the top, especially before dark?*

If she could just rest her eyes for a few minutes, she would have the strength to continue. But just as she closed her eyes, Brogan began barking. Frustrated with Brogan for making so much noise, she opened her eyes to tell him to be quiet. Then she heard a branch crack to the left of her. She turned and to her complete dismay she saw Kavian, the vicious wolf she had so recently shot at Feena's cottage. Her heart was beating so fast she felt like it was in her throat.

Zoe stood up quickly, "What are you doing here?"

"I came to see you. I thought I would give you some helpful hints for your journey," he laughed cruelly.

"I don't need your help. We're doing just fine," she said reaching for her bow.

"There's no need for that!" he said in a mock-injured tone. "I mean you no harm. I just wanted to show you something."

She picked up her bow as she spoke in her most menacing voice. "You have nothing that I want to see. Now leave!"

"Just look behind me. What do you see?"

Zoe could not help but look. When she realized where she was, her mouth dropped open for she saw a path that led from the forest to her little landing. When they reached the landing, she was so tired that she had not taken the time to investigate her surroundings. But she now knew that it was indeed Hemlock Forest just by seeing the deep darkness that penetrated it. To her shock, she realized she could have avoided the rocky road and the first set of cliffs altogether by walking through the forest. Zoe could hardly believe it. Her mind raced with many thoughts. *Why did the King send me this way?*

"Now what do you think about your King? Do you really think He has your best interests in mind? Why would He send you by such a difficult way? Ha! He doesn't care about you. This path is not very far from Feena's cottage. You went the long way to the cliffs. As you can see, you could have easily come this way!"

Zoe looked at the path and then at Kavian, trying to push away doubts about the King. "Well, I'm sure there was a reason for the King sending me the way He did."

"Believe what you like, but I don't think He really wants you to come to His kingdom. You're just a poor orphan with nothing to offer Him."

Zoe felt tears running down her cheeks. "No, you're wrong," she said defensively, but the words even sounded hollow to her.

Kavian began walking toward Brogan, growling menacingly. He was baring his teeth, preparing to attack Brogan at that moment. Before he could, Brogan leaped forward at Kavian. However, the move was ineffective. Kavian flailed him with a tremendous thrust against a rock, and his body fell limply to the ground with a sickening thud. Zoe dropped her bow and ran to him. She leaned her head against his chest to see if he was breathing. He was, but just barely. Zoe had never been so angry. She ran to get her bow, but before she could, Kavian jumped between her and the bow.

"Didn't Feena teach you never to drop your weapon? She really didn't teach you near enough to survive this journey! How foolish you are to believe such dreams! And now there is no one here to help you."

He crept closer as Zoe backed away from him. She did not realize Kavian was backing her to the edge of the cliff. He lunged forward and his blow propelled her body off the edge. As she fell, she heard him yell in triumph, "Ha! This was too easy!" and he retreated back to the woods.

But what Kavian did not stay to see was that Zoe had only fallen about twenty feet and landed safely in some bushes which cushioned her fall. She was cut and bruised, but that was all. Sinking down, she burrowed under the bushes, hiding, not daring to move. She stayed on the ground for a long time, scarcely breathing for fear Kavian might return and discover that she was alive. Time slipped by and finally she decided it would be safe to come out. She was desperate to check on Brogan.

She looked around and saw no sign of Kavian. She realized had she not fallen in these bushes, she would have fallen off the edge of the cliff onto razor sharp rocks far below. Miraculously she was safe. She inched her way up the path only to find Brogan still unconscious.

She checked to see if he was still breathing. He was but he would not wake up when she called his name. *This just cannot be happening!* "Please, please, wake up Brogan. You're going to be fine." She sank to her knees and cried out to the King. "Why did you let this happen? What did he ever do to deserve this?" She sobbed helplessly.

Zoe was again thinking it was a mistake to have come on this journey. Kavian was right. She was nothing but a poor orphan, and definitely not the kind of fighter that such a journey required. Surely the King must not really care about her or Brogan—if He really cared, He never would have let this happen. What was she to do now? If she turned around and went back through the forest to home, Kavian would be sure to find her. She could never leave Brogan anyway. She decided to stay here until she could think about what to do. Hopelessness swept over her and tears fell like rain. She held Brogan in her arms and cried herself into a deep sleep.

She dreamed about being lost in the forest. It was dark and gloomy, for no sunlight could filter through the darkness that surrounded her, which only added to the sad, desperate loneliness she felt. A stranger approached her, and she knew by looking at him that it was Durgalt himself. But because she was so full of despair, she did not have the strength to call for help, and he knew this.

Darkness followed him and he said in a deep voice, "You seem to be lost. Could I help you find your way home?"

Zoe did not want him to think she was afraid, so she calmly said, "I'm just resting. I'll be on my way soon."

"You had better leave—there are wild, dangerous animals in the woods. I just saw a panther no more than five minutes ago!"

She was trying not to shake as she said, "I will leave soon."

His eyes glowered with evil. "What is wrong with you? Don't you realize how dangerous these animals can be? Get up if you value your life!"

Trembling she replied, "I...I...I heard you, and I will...leave soon."

Durgalt gave her a devilish smile and said, "No, you'll be leaving now!"

Zoe tried to speak, but nothing would come out of her mouth. She had no voice! She realized she was in the clutches of her worst enemy, and all she had to do was to call the King to help her, but she could not speak! She tried to run, but he grabbed her by the arm, and pulled her deeper into the forest, farther and farther from where she needed to be.

He laughed, "Did you really think that you could make it to the King's house? You are not fit to go anywhere, but back to the sad little world that you have always known. The King would be here right now to save you—if He really loved you. Face it, no one loves you—not even the King! He has abandoned you, just like your mother!"

He began to laugh wickedly. Zoe at last found her voice and screamed, "No, no, you are wrong! He does love me. I know He does..." She was gasping for breath as fear and despair took control. There is no hope now...

Startled, Zoe felt something wet all over her face. She opened her eyes and caught her breath when she saw Antrum. "It's me, Zoe. Wake up! You're going to be fine. You were just having a bad dream."

"I'm so scared...I don't think I should go on this journey anymore. I cannot do it!" she sobbed.

Then she remembered Brogan. A tear slid down her cheek. "And Brogan, he's dying. Look at him…" her voice trailed off in complete hopelessness.

Antrum went over to Brogan and nudged him. "No, Zoe, Look—he's moving."

A flood of relief spread over Zoe until she saw the blood oozing from a cut on his head. "He's bleeding too much. Antrum, please help him! What can we do?"

But before Antrum could speak, Zoe remembered that she already had just what Brogan needed. "How could I have forgotten? I have some healing balm left from the King's messenger last night!"

She quickly took it out of her bag and lovingly put it on Brogan's cut. It began to close up and in minutes the wound was completely healed. Then she gave him a drink of the King's living water. After he drank, Brogan stood up and wagged his tail as good as new. He covered Zoe's face all over with wet kisses.

Zoe pulled Brogan close to her. "Oh, I'm so glad you're okay, Brogan!"

"Antrum, how did you find me?"

"Evan alerted me. He flies a great distance every day in search of anyone who might need help. Then he brings word to either me or Bantry."

Gratefulness overwhelmed her. "Please, thank him for me."

"I will. He will be pleased that you and Brogan are going to be fine."

Grace, Antrum's mate, walked up to Zoe. "I'm so glad you're not hurt, and you too Brogan."

Antrum looked Zoe over and said, "You're scraped up pretty badly on your face and there is blood on your dress. Are you cut on your legs?"

"Yes, I am, but I'll be all right."

"Would some balm be helpful on your cuts?"

"I'll rub some on the deep cuts, especially this one on my face, but I want to save as much of this ointment as I can for I do not know when we will need it next."

"What happened to you anyway?"

Zoe told Antrum and Grace the whole story, and then her dream. Antrum said, "If you don't mind, may I give you a bit of advice?"

"Why yes, of course!"

"First of all, you should not have even talked to Kavian. He was up to no good from the beginning. Remember, he's your enemy, not a friend. Never listen to the enemy's voice. Also, you should not have put down your bow even when Brogan was hurt. You let your guard down and he took advantage of it, almost killing you."

Stung, Zoe said, "You are right Antrum. I wasn't thinking. He came upon me so suddenly. Please, can you tell me more about Durgalt? I have to know who I am up against." Zoe shuddered as she thought about the ugly face she had seen in her dream.

"He is the leader of all the wicked creatures and humans on the earth. He is devious in every imaginable way and he will stop at nothing to get you and others to turn away from following the King. He may be hard to detect at times because he can have the face of so many creatures."

"I didn't know that. In my dream, he looked human, but he seemed to have some features of a ferocious animal. He had fangs, horns, and a lot of dark hair on his face and hands. I could not see the rest of his body because he wore pants and a shirt."

Antrum continued, "I am certain that was him. Zoe, listen to me. Sooner or later you will come face to face with him and many of his evil followers. Remember that every time they attack you it is a chance for you to defeat them. You must learn to seize these opportunities, and view them as such.

"Your dream was an attack but you can use it as a warning. It has revealed the lies that the enemy is trying to plant in your heart. If you listen to him, you will fall into the deadly trap of despair. His words echoed in your mind as you slept because he knows your fears and insecurities, and he will try to use them all against you. He is a wise and devious foe, but if you will not lose your trust in the King, you can turn every one of Durgalt's attacks into a victory over your fears.

"When you became hopeless, you opened the door for the enemy to torment you. If you had continued to trust the King, even in this, Durgalt would have left you alone. The last place he wants to be is close to someone who is living in the peace that comes to those who trust the King. You recently received the **Key to Peace**. Use it! It is a key to your victory."

Zoe reached in her pocket and touched the key. "You are so right Antrum. Zoe hung her head low. "I failed this test miserably."

Compassionately Antrum said, "I will not lie to you. You did not pass this test, but you will have the chance to take it again. You are still learning, and you do know more now, but you still have much to learn yet. It is important to learn from your mistakes so that you do not repeat them again. Remember to stand on what you know to be true—the King loves you and He will take care of you! He asked you to go on this journey. Did you think to call on Him to help you?"

"I didn't think He loved or cared for me anymore because of what happened to us. I just could not understand why He sent me on that horrible cliff when I could have walked up from the forest."

"Zoe, for you to succeed you must understand that you are not given hardships because He does not love you, but because He does. He called you because He has great faith in you. He has a purpose in everything. You must be tested. The only way to pass the test is to trust and obey Him in every area of your life—even when you do not understand why certain things happen. You must never doubt that He loves you and has your best interest in mind in everything that He allows in your life. It is hard at times, but if it were not hard, you would not grow. You are not on this journey because you are ready, but to make you ready." Antrum's eyes softened. "Everything is going to be fine. You will see."

"Look, it is already dark. I was sent to bring you to the clearing to recuperate and gain new strength. You will be safe there. And just think, you are already one level up. You only have to climb two more cliffs. Now come along and we will find something to eat."

*Greater trust in Him builds
greater faith in Him.*

Chapter Ten

Trust in the LORD with all your heart,
and do not lean on your own understanding.
In all your ways acknowledge Him,
and He will make your paths straight.
Proverbs 3:5-6

Zoe watched as the sun began to peek above the horizon. An overnight rain caused the branches on the trees to sparkle like jewels, as they hovered over the clearing like a huge canopy. Bluebirds were singing a joyful song and the squirrels twitched their tails in curiosity while playfully running back and forth among the leaves. Her eyes wandered to the exquisite shades of purple and pink flowers that grew randomly in the forest. As she bent down to smell them, Grace, Antrum's mate, quietly approached Zoe with a radiant smile on her face.

"You know Zoe, each of these flowers have their own particular scent and beauty—it is their purpose. Just like the flowers, you have a purpose too, a destiny. This is what you must find."

Antrum walked up and nuzzled Grace on the neck while Zoe gazed at the flowers. "The only purpose that I know I have is to reach Remiah. But somehow I feel like there must be more. I hope I'll discover what it is on this journey." Zoe smiled. "I wish I could visit longer, but Brogan and I need to climb the remaining cliffs before sunset. It was so good to rest in such peace. Thank you for everything. I will always be grateful."

Antrum replied, "Just stay on the path, trust in the King, and you will be fine."

"I will." Zoe waved goodbye and began following the path back to the cliffs, thankful that she did not have to start at the bottom again. She fought to overcome the swell of fear that was rising up within her as she looked at the massive rock ledges.

"Come here Brogan, I have to tie this rope around you and then tie you to my back—this is just too steep and I fear you'll fall."

When the rope was secure around Brogan, Zoe began the dangerous climb up the second cliff. Each step was tedious. and Brogan became heavier with each step she took. Her heart began to beat faster and harder. As she struggled to climb, her strength was leaving.

Then the path through the cliffs became even more narrow so that Zoe had to walk sideways and lean against the large rocks that lined the inside of the path. It was agonizing just to maintain her balance, but finally she was through the narrow pass. Then to her dismay the path led right to the edge of the cliff. As she took the next step, a rock crumbled causing her to stumble and lose balance. Brogan whimpered as she crushed him against the rocks. One of her legs was hanging off the side of the precipice, while she fought with all her strength to hold on to the other side of the cliff. As her fingers dug into the rocks and dirt, they began to bleed. She desperately grabbed a rock that was protruding, and slowly began to pull herself and Brogan back up. Finally, they were safely on the next landing. She untied Brogan, but could do nothing but lay flat on her stomach from exhaustion. Her leg and arm muscles felt like jelly.

Tears fell when she realized that she and Brogan had almost been killed, again. *I cannot do this! It is impossible!* Brogan began licking her face. She opened her eyes and then gazed deeply into his eyes as he tenderly looked at her. It seemed to reawaken the responsibility of getting the two of them safely to the top.

She sat up, looked in her bag and found the water, took a swallow, and then gave some to Brogan. She looked at her hands and saw there were deep gashes. She washed them off with the water as best she could, but decided against using the healing balm. They would heal soon enough and the ointment was too precious to use for her cuts and abrasions. They ate some wafers and cheese and soon both felt better.

The day was beautiful, but it did nothing to remove the dread that filled Zoe when she looked at the final cliff above her. She just wanted to get this over with and continue on her journey. She stood on trembling legs, checked to make sure the rope was securely tied around Brogan, and took the next step on the final cliff leading to four hours of fighting desperately just to maintain their balance while inching their way up. Finally, after all her strength was expended, and she felt she could not take one more step, she saw the top. Zoe breathed a sigh of relief. With every ounce of strength she could muster, she steadily worked her way to the plateau. She untied Brogan, set him down, and fell on her back in total exhaustion. Brogan was so glad to get untied that he jumped around ecstatically.

After resting a few minutes, Zoe surveyed the landing. There were rocks of all sizes and there was a clearing with a patch of grass that would do nicely for them to rest for the night.

"Are you hungry, Brogan? Come here, let me see what we can find in my bag." She pulled out some bread, cheese, and fruit that Feena had given them and they devoured it quickly. Zoe was still so tired from the climb that she did not even bother to get her mat and blanket out. She leaned against a huge boulder and closed her eyes. Brogan put his head on her lap and they both fell fast asleep until early morning when the bright sunshine awakened them.

"Well, fella, we better eat something," she said to a bright eyed Brogan. On the small landing, Zoe picked some blackberries from the bushes that amazingly grew there. She ate them with the last of the bread. Brogan was not thrilled with the blackberries, but he gobbled the bread.

Zoe was so tired the night before that she had not looked at the surroundings in great detail. She saw a forest and as she checked the map she felt that this must be Runden Forest. Then her heart sank. This was the enemy's forest! Feena, however had said that her friends the elves, occupied part of the forest. But what part? She was still very tired and sore from the strenuous climb. How could she face her enemies in this condition? She needed more rest. *Why was this journey so hard?* Finally, she resolved that she had made it this far, so the sooner they began, the sooner they would get through this forest.

"Come on Brogan. We might as well get started."

This place reminded her of Hemlock Forest—creepy, dark, and cold. She put on her cape and buttoned it. The path took them straight into the deepest part of the forest. The wind seemed to be whispering strange words. Then she realized that it was the gruelas again! Their dark shadows appeared in front, behind, and beside her. Brogan barked constantly trying to ward off the spooky shadows, but they continued to swarm. Zoe breathed deeply and determined not to let fear overcome her. Then the gruelas began screaming their horrible shrieks, making both Zoe and Brogan tremble. "I will not be afraid! I will not be afraid!" She kept repeating this over and over.

As they moved in closer, she took out her bow and shot at the one in front of her. The arrow went right through it and it continued to move in closer. "Oh my King, help me!"

At the mention of the King's name, they let out a skriek and flew away. With amazement, Zoe sat down and looked around. "Look Brogan, they're gone. They are more afraid of the King's name than we are of them. You can be sure I will remember that in the future!"

Their walk remained uneventful for the next few hours, which enabled them to make serious progress. As they sat down to rest and eat, Zoe noticed that soon they would be completely out of food. They shared a few wafers and nuts, which tasted like a feast because they were both so famished.

"We need to keep moving, Brogan. Maybe we can get through this forest before dark." Zoe felt more doubtful the longer they walked. She had so hoped that she would see Feena's friends, the elves, before now. They walked until it was almost dark and then Zoe saw a cave off the path to the left.

Let's stop here for the night, Brogan." As they stepped near and peered into the cave, it emitted a strange, rotten smell so strong that it made Zoe's eyes water. Nevertheless, they decided to stay because they had not seen any other shelter. Zoe was just going to lay her things down when she heard a growl that sent shivers up her spine. Brogan began smelling to see where the odor and growl were coming from. He did not have to search far.

There was not one, but five of the ugliest creatures Zoe had ever seen. She stood up and backed against the cave wall. Brogan growled and bared his teeth. The creatures stood on two feet with boar-like heads and fangs that extended almost to their chins. Their eyes were blood-shot and their drool was so putrid that Zoe gagged. They stood about eight feet tall with matted fur and claws that were extended, ready to flay their victims. As the largest of the creatures started inching toward Zoe, she could see the evil intent in his eyes.

She reached for her bow but he pushed her hand down, grabbed her around the waist, and lifted her high in the air. Brogan bit the creature furiously on the leg. With a terrifying scream, it attempted to grab Brogan, dropping Zoe to the ground. It tried to snatch her again, but Zoe grabbed her bow, pulled out an arrow, aimed, and shot him in the chest. He fell to the ground with a loud thud. When he did not move, a great fury ensued from the remaining four creatures.

"Come on Brogan! Run—it's our only chance!"

They ran out of the cave opening into the forest, not knowing where they were going. They could hear the creatures close behind them, and if that was not bad enough, gruelas began appearing everywhere. Zoe and Brogan ran as fast as they could. Fortunately, the ugly boar-like creatures were cumbersome and slow and could not keep up with them. Even so, the gruelas were now surrounding Zoe and Brogan, filling their minds with horrible fears, thoughts, and doubts. She could hear their voices whispering in her ear, "You will never get away from them…you will soon die. Give up…give up."

In the blackness of night it seemed much easier to believe them than to fight any more. With all the strength she had left, Zoe pushed back those thoughts and prayed for help. Then she screamed, "Somebody help! I'm Feena's friend!" No sooner had she said those words when she ran straight into the powerful arms of a young man.

"Please, help us. They're right behind us! They'll be here any second!"

He grabbed her arm and pushed her forward. "Quickly, climb up here. You'll be safe." Rope steps seemed to appear out of nowhere. They led upward into a huge oak tree. Brogan and Zoe climbed up to the landing in the tree and then someone hurriedly pulled the steps up.

The four hideously fanged creatures soon appeared at the edge of the thicket, but guards appeared standing in their way. The leader yelled, "Give us the girl and the wolf. They invaded our territory and killed one of our triblens. She must die for this."

Her rescuer stepped forward. "No, she is now under our protection. Leave now, Crendor, or you will pay a similar price!"

Crendor's clawed hands were opening and closing while he was contemplating what to do. "Arden, you know the law of our land. When someone is killed unjustly, another must die in his place. Are you denying this?"

"No, I do not deny that this is the law. But we've only heard your side. Let us now hear what the girl has to say."

He turned to Zoe. "Please, do not be frightened. I must know what happened."

Zoe stepped into the light. "We did go into their cave, but we were only looking for shelter for the night. One of the triblens attacked me and I shot him with my bow out of self-defense. I did not mean for him to die or even be injured. I am so sorry." Tears were streaming down Zoe's face.

Arden compassionately laid his hand on her shoulder and then turned to Crendor. "She is telling the truth. You know the law does not apply to self-defense. She is free to stay with us now. You, however, must leave."

Crendor exploded in rage. "You cannot believe this girl over my word! You elves think you know everything—you do not know her!"

"No, I don't, but I can discern that she is telling the truth. You, on the other hand, are known to be a liar and deceiver. This is the last time I will ask you to leave. Now go." The guards pointed their spears at Crendor and the three other triblens.

"Do you think you will win this easily? You best be watching your back, Arden. We will get that girl, and you too. You cannot deny us justice without paying the price yourself."

"With you around I always watch my back, and I am sure that justice was served already tonight. Perhaps much more is due you, which we will gladly administer if you do not leave!"

Crendor spit on the ground and cursed as he walked away.

Zoe was relieved as she watched Crendor leave, and thankful for the wisdom that Arden had used to handle this situation. So he was an elf! He was much taller than she thought an elf would be. Zoe was a little over five feet, and he was slightly over six feet. He was young, muscular, and very handsome with curly, blond hair and a tan complexion. She could only stare at his beautiful eyes—light blue and gentle, yet revealing unwavering strength and resolve. His only elf-like feature were his ears, and they were only slightly pointed.

He turned to Zoe and saw that she was staring at him. Their eyes met and something happened between them—something Zoe had never felt before. She turned away for she did not understand this feeling, but his gaze never left her. "Let me introduce myself. I'm Arden."

She faced him again shyly. "My name is Zoe."

"I received word from a friend of mine that you would be traveling through Runden Forest on your way to Remiah. You are quite young to be making this trip alone."

"I'm not that young—I'm eighteen, and Brogan is with me."

Arden bent down to look at Brogan. "A fine wolf he is, and I am sure a fine friend too." Brogan wagged his tail. "You are welcome to stay with us for as long as you wish. I feel certain that you could use some rest."

"Thank you sir. I would be pleased to stay the night. I cannot imagine going back out into that forest again in the dark."

With a bit of hesitation in his voice, he looked at her strangely and replied, "There is much to say, but I can see you are exhausted. We will wait and talk in the morning."

Arden turned and called a young elf. "Mara, please see that Zoe is taken to the cottage by the lake and help her get settled for the night."

"I will be most honored to help this young maiden, Prince Arden." Turning to Zoe she said, "Please, follow me."

Zoe turned to Arden. "You're a Prince?"

Smiling, he answered. "Yes. My father, the King of the elves has been away serving another group of elves until their leader recovers from a wound. So I am our leader until he returns. Sleep peacefully for our land is well guarded. I look forward to our talk in the morning." Zoe felt herself blushing as he touched her cheek.

"Thank you so much for your kindness. You saved my life. I will try not to be any more trouble." Zoe curtsied and followed Mara.

Arden watched as Zoe and Brogan walked away. What was it about this young maiden that intrigued him so? True, her beauty was rare with a face that lit up the night and lovely long brown hair that swayed with her every move. But it was the sincerity in her eyes of golden brown that had touched his heart. She looked so gentle, yet she had fought the triblens alone and even killed one. He marveled as he thought about how lovely and wonderful this girl was. Then the thought struck him so hard that it took his breath away! Could she be the fulfillment of the prophecy spoken by his father just a year before? He had to find it and read it again. Already he was quite sure that she might just be the one!

❋

Zoe and Brogan followed Mara past cascading waterfalls and dozens of yellow marigolds that glowed in the moonlight. As she walked, she could not stop thinking about Prince Arden. He was unlike anyone she had ever met—strong, self-assured, but not arrogant. He was breathtakingly handsome and kind. Why did she blush when he touched her? He said they would talk in the morning. Perhaps some of her questions about him would be answered then.

Suddenly the difficult climb and terrors in the forest all seemed to have been well worth it. How could she have ever lived without such adventure in her life? As tired as she was, she felt more alive than ever before. She could not wait until morning to learn more about the elves, and especially Prince Arden.

Faith means to trust, confidently believing.

Chapter Eleven

I will lie down and sleep in peace,
for you alone, O LORD, make me dwell in safety.
Psalm 4:8 (NIV)

Zoe awoke feeling totally refreshed. As she sat up in bed, she saw that Mara was still by her side and wondered if she had watched over her all night. Her eyes wandered around the little cottage and realized that it was very much like her own. It felt good here. There was a nice, warm fire in the stone fireplace that was very comforting, which was much more pleasant than spending the night in a cave! She was so relaxed that the hard climb and trek through the forest seemed a distant memory.

"Mara, from what I have seen of Runden Forest, it is quite beautiful. Have you lived here long?"

She turned to face Zoe. "Oh yes. I have lived here all my life."

"You must have enjoyed a lovely childhood."

"Yes I did. Thank you," she said shyly.

"Mara, I was just wondering—where is Prince Arden's mother? He spoke only of his father."

Mara's countenance completely changed to that of deep sadness. "Just two years ago, she was befriended by a strange woman in the forest. This woman was very beautiful, but as we sadly discovered too late, she was quite evil on the inside. During one of their visits, the woman gave Queen Enda a poisonous tea, which she innocently drank. Immediately the Queen became sick. We gave her many types of herbs in hopes of curing her, but nothing helped. She quietly died in Prince Arden's arms within hours of receiving the poison. King Ronan had been away at a council meeting and when he arrived home that evening, he was completely shocked to discover that his Queen had died that after-noon. I have never seen a more devastated man. She was the kind-est person I have ever known and we all still miss her dearly."

"But why would that woman do such a terrible thing?"

"She was on a mission sent by Durgalt to kill Queen Enda. She was a witch, Zoe."

Zoe gasped. "I didn't know there were real witches. The stories I have heard gave me the impression they were ugly old hags."

"Oh, no. Witches can be quite beautiful, as she was. I am quite certain there are ugly witches and warlocks for that matter, but this one fooled everyone because of her beauty and the appearance of being very kind. We are born with the gift of discernment, but we were still fooled. Since then, we have all prayed for our discernment to grow so that we will not be fooled again. We must grow in the ways of the King so that our light will outshine this growing darkness. If we do not—the evil will overcome us."

"I know you are quite right Mara. Did you find the woman who killed Queen Enda?" Zoe asked.

"Yes we did. She met her death recently when she tried to kill Prince Arden. He heard a noise behind him, and when he turned he knocked a knife out of her hand, which cut her as it fell to the ground. It was but a tiny wound, but she had put a deadly poison on it. She died from her own poison, which seemed most appropriate. I think in the end all witches die from their own evil. The law of the land says that we will all reap what we sow, and they are ultimately the victims of their own evil ways."

"It seems they would learn."

"Wisdom is clouded by evil. Evil is darkness and it is hard to see in the dark."

"You certainly seem to be a deep well of wisdom," Zoe re-sponded, a bit uncomfortable with the respect being shown to her by such a regal young lady as Mara.

Mara smiled. "You are too kind."

"I speak the truth Mara. But I will say that I am so thankful that Prince Arden was not stabbed!" Zoe offered, catching herself lest she seem too captivated by him, while in her heart she knew that she certainly was.

"We are also. She is just one of many witches who serve Durgalt, and they are scattered throughout the land. We will pray for your protection from them."

"Thank you. I am most grateful."

Zoe marveled at the sincerity she had detected in Mara's lovely face. Zoe watched her as she moved gracefully about the cottage straightening the beds and sweeping. She could be no more than her own age of eighteen. Her long blond hair shone as if it had been freshly washed and her clear blue eyes glowed with kindness. Zoe knew that Mara was very special indeed. Perhaps one day, if she ever returned to Runden Forest, she could develop a closer friendship with her.

Mara asked if Zoe would like to take a walk and then bathe. "The water is such a refreshing temperature this time of year."

"That is a fine idea, Mara."

Mara bent down to pick up a branch that had fallen from the tree and moved it aside so they could walk. Brogan enjoyed the romp and playfully grabbed a stick for Zoe to throw to him. They played the stick game while they walked, then Zoe focused her attention on Mara.

"How long have you been serving Prince Arden and his family?"

"Oh, my mother was dear friends with Queen Enda, and they both passed away within weeks of each other—it was quite strange. I choose to serve King Ronan and his family because I love them so much. It is my desire to serve them as best I can."

"You are very giving Mara, and I would consider it an honor if you would be my friend."

Mara curtsied, "It is I who will have the honor, m'lady."

Their conversation flowed as if they had known each other all of their lives. "I hope I will meet King Ronan some day."

Mara smiled. "I believe one day you will. He is a wonderful leader and very compassionate."

Zoe wondered if she should ask, thinking it might be a little forward, but her curiosity was so great that she just had to know.

She cleared her throat and asked. "Mara, could you tell me about Prince Arden?"

"He is a just and kind leader like his father. Prince Arden always puts the welfare of his people first—whether it regards safety, provision, or our spiritual condition. My people love him as we love his father."

Zoe thought to herself that she liked Prince Arden more and more. Certainly these elves were truly noble beings.

When they reached the lake, she bathed and swam for a few minutes and then dressed quickly because her stomach was alerting her that it was time to eat.

When they walked back to the cabin, an abundant provision of food was set on the table for breakfast and Zoe ate heartily. She noticed that Brogan had also been provided for as well.

Mara turned to Zoe. "Prince Arden said that you are welcome to stay here as long as you wish. You can ring this bell when you need something for I will be attending to you. "

"You are quite thoughtful and I thank you for your kindness," Zoe said.

"We have all been commanded to see that you get as much rest as possible. Have you eaten enough?"

"Oh yes, I don't know when food has tasted so good. I would like to thank whoever prepared this breakfast, but I do not see anyone to thank."

"Your just being here is thanks enough. We love visitors, and it's hard for all of the elves to stay away as we especially love to hear the stories of those who are passing through on their journey."

Zoe felt so important—she had never felt that way before. She sat down to enjoy the crackling fire, feeling full of peace. Although she had slept late and had just eaten a wonderful breakfast, she could not help herself from nodding off to sleep. Her dreams were so wonderful that when she awoke she wanted to fall back to sleep, which she did over and over.

Rest comes easily to those who live in peace.

Chapter Twelve

"Put me like a seal over your heart, like a seal on your arm.
For love is as strong as death."
Song of Solomon 8:6

Arden had something very important to share with Zoe, but he refrained from visiting her until later in the morning, knowing she needed her rest. When he could wait no longer, he walked the short distance to her cottage and knocked on the door. No one answered. He saw Mara hanging out clothes to dry. "Is Zoe still resting?"

"She was, but now she is by the waterfall, Prince Arden."

"Thank you, Mara." As Arden approached the waterfall he could hear Zoe laughing. He stood at a distance behind some bushes and watched her play with Brogan. He was amazed at her beauty and sweetness. As he began walking toward her, suddenly Evan landed beside him.

"Evan, my friend, it's so good to see you this morning. Thank you for bringing the news to me about Zoe. She has arrived here safely, but I greatly fear she is in now in perilous danger with Crendor."

"Yes, I heard about the incident last night, but she is safe for now." Evan looked hard at Arden. "But what is this I see in your eyes?"

Arden paused as in deep thought. "There have been many young maidens that have passed through our land, yet none have touched my heart the way Zoe has. Do you recall the prophecy that my father gave me?"

"Please, my friend, refresh my memory."

"He spoke of a maiden who would come by night seeking refuge and that I would rescue her. Also he mentioned that she would be a rare beauty. He said she would be on a journey, and that we would be separated for a time but reunited in the next season. Evan, when I first looked at her, I was immediately drawn to her and I believe she is the fulfillment of the prophecy. I did indeed rescue her last night, she is a rare beauty, and she is on a journey, but these are not the only reasons I feel she is to be my bride—my heart tells me she is the one! How can I let her go so soon after meeting her? Especially since her life is in great danger."

Evan stretched his wings and then walked closer to Arden. "As I learned from Feena, the King has called Zoe on a journey to Remiah. She has to go, Arden—it is her destiny. She will be changed and be all the more prepared to take her place as Princess if she is indeed the one. To deny her this journey would be wrong. As you well know, it takes faith *and* patience to inherit the promises from the King. If she is the one, she will be worth the wait, but wait you must."

"This does not make it any easier."

"Arden, she is a skilled archer and has endured several battles with Kavian. She is a strong woman, though she does not seem to know it yet. Even with the added danger of Crendor, we cannot stop her from going to Remiah."

Arden knew Evan was right. "I agree, but I must talk to her about the perils that she will surely meet."

As he said those words, Zoe approached with Brogan following. Arden caught his breath at the sight of her.

"Good morning Prince Arden and Evan." She curtsied. "I am so glad to see you."

The elegance with which she walked, her delicate features, and the locks of hair falling gracefully to her waist, overwhelmed Arden. He was afraid of embarrassing himself because he could not take his eyes off of her. As he stared, her lovely smile did strange things to his heart. He was so captivated that he could not speak.

Evan broke the silence. "We are glad to see you too. You look radiant this morning."

"Thank you, Evan. It is from the wonderful rest and swim from earlier. I have not felt this peaceful and safe since I left my own little cottage."

She continued, "Prince Arden is not only my rescuer, but his hospitality has revived me." Their eyes met and Evan began to feel he was intruding on a special moment, so he felt it was time to leave.

"We're quite glad you are rested now. Zoe, I wanted to say goodbye for I must go on urgent business for Feena. I am sure our paths will meet again soon."

Her eyes expressed a longing that intrigued Arden even more. "Oh, how I miss Feena. How is she doing?"

"Quite wonderful and busy as usual."

"Evan, please give her my love when you see her. Oh, and thank you so much for telling Arden that I was coming through Runden Forest. I don't know what I would have done without everyone's help. I will always be grateful."

"I was honored to help and I will help you more as I can in the future. I must take my leave for now. A wonderful and safe journey to you, Zoe." And with those words he flew away.

Mara called Brogan to come eat something special that she had made for him, which left Zoe and Arden standing alone.

"Forgive me Zoe for staring, but I am overwhelmed with your beauty."

Zoe blushed and looked down. "Thank you Prince Arden," she stammered, feeling completely awkward as she never considered herself beautiful before or important.

Arden smiled and touched her cheek. "Will you take a walk with me and talk for a while?"

"Yes, I would like that."

Arden was unsure where to begin for his heart wanted to share so much with Zoe. "I understand from Evan that you are going to Remiah."

"Yes and it has already been an amazing journey. I wanted adventure and I have certainly had it! It has been both the best and the hardest thing that I have ever done, but already it is well worth it."

Arden smiled knowingly. "I made the journey two years ago, right after my mother's death."

Zoe was not surprised. "Mara told me about your mother. I am so sorry about her untimely death."

"Thank you Zoe. It was the hardest thing emotionally that I have ever been through. The pain is beginning to ease now, though I still miss her greatly."

Zoe looked at him as if she could understand his pain. "Arden, I thought you had made the journey to Remiah. You not only have great leadership abilities but you are compassionate and wise far beyond your years. When I thought about you this morning I felt that only the intensity of the journey to Remiah could develop such character in one at such a young age."

"Twenty-one is young, but I've had to grow up more quickly than most due to responsibilities in our kingdom here. But thank you Zoe." He took her hands. The moment became so intense that the Prince felt that he had to say something.

"I do not want to frighten you Zoe, but Crendor will not forget what happened to Futney, the triblen that died. I know him very well, and he will seek revenge." For a moment Arden was sorry that he had brought up such a dark subject, but then he quickly knew it was right, and that Zoe's life might well depend on her understanding the reality of what was indeed a serious danger.

"I thought as much, too."

He brushed a lock of hair off her cheek. "I want to ensure your safety. Will you allow me to go with you on the remainder of your journey?"

"Oh, Prince Arden. I am honored that you want to protect me, but I am not alone for I have Brogan with me. And your responsibilities here are too vast to leave and go with me. As much as I would enjoy your company, I feel that this journey is just for Brogan and me at this time."

"Please, call me Arden. You are right of course, but I just cannot bear the thought of someone trying to harm you."

Questioningly, Zoe replied. "You hardly know me, Arden."

"That is true, Zoe, but I feel a very special connection to you already."

Zoe continued. "As you know, the King called me on this journey, so I am under His protection."

"Of course, and He is certainly able to keep you, Zoe, but we must still use wisdom. Would you mind if I sent Evan to follow your course and then I could check on you from time to time?"

Zoe smiled. "I would like that very much. I can also show you the map the King gave me. Perhaps you can give me some helpful insights."

"Yes, I would like to look at it and make a copy."

Arden cleared his throat and seemed yet again at a loss for words as he looked at the light reflecting the amber flecks of her extraodinary eyes.

"I have never met anyone like you. Though your beauty is astounding, this is not all that has drawn me to you—I feel a special bond between us as I just mentioned."

Zoe looked into his clear, blue eyes. "I've felt this too, but I was not sure what it was, and I also didn't want to be presumptuous. You are, after all, a Prince and I am but a commoner."

"Zoe, everyone called by the King is noble. You are on the journey to take your place in His royal family. All who finish the journey become royalty. You must not think of yourself as a commoner any longer. I do not mean to assume your feelings are the same as mine, but I feel we have a destiny together—something very special."

Arden was still holding her hands. Zoe looked deeper into his eyes and realized that perhaps this was true—it was no accident they had met, but she wanted to be sure.

"Arden, a destiny together?"

He hesitated. "I mean Zoe, that I believe you are the one I am to marry."

Zoe's eyes widened. For a moment she wondered if she had somehow fallen back to sleep and she was still dreaming. She had never been captivated by anyone before, so she had to catch her breath.

"Arden, I think you must be the most wonderful person I have ever met, and yes, I feel a bond between us too, but marriage? How can you say such a thing so soon?"

"Zoe, search your heart." As they looked deeply into each other's eyes, Zoe felt as if she were falling off a cliff, and she had to catch herself. She prayed that the King would show her if he was the one for her. It just seemed too wonderful. How could she ever even dream that she could marry a Prince, much less a Prince of the elves?

"What are you thinking, Zoe?"

She hesitated. "What makes you think we should be together?"

"You are the one in the prophecy that my father gave me and I feel this confirmed in my heart."

"Prophecy?"

Arden told Zoe about the prophecy. She had to sit down on a nearby stump to steady herself and think about it. Finally she spoke. "I can see why you would think it's me, Arden, and though I find you more than fascinating and handsome, I will need some time to think about this. How can you be certain that it is not someone else?"

"I have never been more confident of anything in my life."

Zoe rubbed her temples as if she was trying to clear everything out of her mind so she could see the way Arden did. After what seemed like an eternity to Arden, she spoke. "Arden, I hardly know you. If this is meant to be, can you give it some time? As much as I want this to be true, for some reason my heart is not sure. Perhaps we should see how we feel after my journey."

Zoe could not believe what she had just said. She had a chance to be Arden's wife and yet she did not say yes! She was certain he would be the most wonderful husband ever, so what was lacking that she could not give him her heart?

Arden could not hide his disappointment "Yes, of course, Zoe, but there will never be anyone else for me but you, and I will wait as long as it takes." He sat down beside her and put his arm around her. Zoe did not move but enjoyed his embrace and eventually put her head on his shoulder.

Gently, Arden released her. "It will be one of the hardest days of my life when you leave Zoe, but I know you must go to Remiah. I also know the King will protect you. But you must realize that I will come to help anytime you need me."

"Thank you Arden." She reached up and touched his blond curls. "I have been wanting to do that ever since I met you!"

"You may do that anytime you desire, Zoe!" He took her in his arms again and held her. Reluctantly, he released her and they began walking back to her cottage, hand in hand.

They spent the rest of the afternoon talking. She showed him the map and he gave her warnings that she was certain would prove of great help to her. The afternoon slipped into evening and they ate a quiet dinner together. Sadness draped over them as they both knew that tomorrow Zoe would be continuing on her journey, so they savored their time together.

"I was wondering Arden, why do you live in this forest when you are surrounded by so much evil?"

"We choose to do this for several reasons. This has been our home for generations, and we want to hold on to it for the King. We could have moved away, but we know that some day all of the forest will belong to the King again. He could lay claim to it at anytime, but right now He is giving the triblens more time to stop following Durgalt, and return to Him. Soon their time will be up."

Zoe contemplated the whole situation. "If by then, they have not chosen to follow the King, will there be a battle among the elves and the triblens?"

"Yes, but my hope is that they will turn to the King."

"I do too, Arden. They are fierce, but I feel pity for them. They live in such a dark place. Can they see the difference in how they live and how the elves live?"

"They do, but it only makes them jealous and bitter. They think we have stolen all that we have from them, so they try to steal all that they can from us."

Zoe yawned though she was anything but bored. Arden took her in his arms, and held her for a long time. He gently brushed her hair away from her face. "I must go now for it is late. Sleep well, my Princess." And with those words he said goodnight and walked back to his cottage.

⊷⚹⊶

Zoe woke up and looked around. Brogan was still asleep for it was early in the morning. She quietly tiptoed out of the cottage and went down to the lake to swim. Today she was leaving Runden Forest and Arden—how hard it would be.

She sat in the sun until her hair was just slightly damp from the swim. She walked back to her cottage only to find Arden sitting under the willow tree by her door. "I was getting a little impatient waiting for you. Are you hungry?"

"Yes, I am, but…"

"What is it Zoe?"

Zoe sat down on a nearby log and held her knees tightly to her chest. "I was hoping we might have a little time together alone, so we could talk."

Arden pulled her up and took her in his arms. "I know, and we will have time to talk after we eat."

Zoe smiled. "All right then, let's go.

A large table was set up in the shade of the trees, laden with fruit, eggs, scones, honey, cheese, and all kinds of juices. In total twenty elves were at the breakfast. After everyone had finished eating, Arden tapped his glass to get everyone's attention. "My friends, thank you for this wonderful breakfast. I would like to introduce you to Zoe, who is very special to me."

She blushed as he said this. Arden extended his hand for her to stand beside him. "Zoe is on her way to Remiah, and she will need our prayers. As you know, Crendor may try to follow her, attempting to get revenge for the death of Futney. Evan has agreed to check on her and keep me posted of her progress. If he informs me that she needs help, I will leave immediately. I know many of our friends could not be here this morning, so please notify them of this."

Arden continued. "Zoe and I must talk now, but again thank you for the excellent breakfast and for being such loyal friends."

"And we thank you for being such an excellent leader," one of the elves responded. "That which is important to our Prince is important to us all. We too will be ready to leave immediately to help you or Zoe."

Everyone spoke to Zoe and Arden before they left, pledging their prayers would be with her.

Arden took Zoe's hand and pulled her toward the stables. "Do you know how to ride a horse?"

"Yes, my aunt had horses and I rode quite often."

"Good, because I am giving you one to ride on your journey." Zoe started to refuse.

"I know what you're going to say, Zoe, but this is something I want to do for you. All who take the journey must learn to receive the help the King sends to us through those He places on our path. You will not be so tired on your journey if you can ride and you will arrive in Remiah sooner than if you had to walk. Brogan will also enjoy the faster pace, believe me."

"I do not know what to say Arden, except thank you. This is quite unexpected and I am grateful—I will return the horse to you as soon as I can."

"No, she is a gift to you. You know how I feel about you Zoe, and I want to do everything to ensure that you return to me safely." They walked up to a beautiful mare that was solid white. "This is Dapple. She is young, just two years old, and of a calm disposition. She is obedient and one of my fastest horses."

Zoe lifted her hand to pat her nose and Dapple nuzzled closer to her. "She is wonderful. Thank you so much." She reached up and kissed Arden on the cheek. Arden pulled Zoe to him and held her, wondering when he would see her again.

"I asked Mara to pack an abundance of food for you. She should be here with it soon. As much as I do not want you to go, the sooner you leave, the sooner you will return to me. This journey has already changed your life, I'm sure, and it will change even more as you complete the task. Treasure every part of it."

They walked back to the cottage and gathered Zoe's things. They embraced one last time and then Arden helped Zoe climb up on Dapple. She turned, waved, and then she and Brogan were off once again on their adventure.

Arden stood staring at Zoe as she found the path. His heart went with her, and he would pray constantly for the King to watch over her. He had already contacted Evan about her leaving, to keep him informed of her progress, and of any danger. Arden also knew that the nature of the journey was that most of the danger would come in a way where he would not be able to help her, and she would have to face it herself. Arden now felt that he was going to have to trust the King even more for Zoe's journey than he did for his own.

His biggest concern was Crendor, but then, what about Kavian? Kavian thought she was dead, but he would soon find out differently. Crendor was her immediate threat. Even though the King sentenced him years ago to never leave Runden Forest, Arden knew Crendor and his evil ways—he would stop at nothing to get revenge. If he found out that Zoe might be the fulfillment of the prophecy, he would be even more determined. The King's enemies knew that few things strengthened His people more than seeing prophecies fulfilled.

Unknown to Arden, Crendor was in fact well aware of this prophecy, and he thought when he saw Zoe in the cave that she was the one. He also knew the wrath of Durgalt would know no limits if he let her make it through the forest. His spies had watched her every minute, and they were waiting for her to get just far enough from Arden's reach to make their move.

Promises will be fulfilled with faith and patience.

Part IV
The Journey

Chapter Thirteen

*But the Lord is faithful, and He will strengthen
and protect you from the evil one.
II Thessalonians 3:3*

To Zoe, Arden seemed like a dream that was just too good to be true. How could a seamstress marry a Prince? Then again, she could never imagine herself making such an extra-ordinary journey. Maybe this was the beginning of an extraordinary life in which even marrying a Prince was possible.

Laying those thoughts aside, she realized she needed to focus on the task ahead—her next destination—Dunrow Desert. The thought of traveling through a desert was not something she was looking forward to, but she did have Dapple to ride and that would make her journey easier. Brogan was with her and he was a great comfort, too.

She traveled for many miles without any sign of a desert. The fields were blooming abundantly with wildflowers of every shade. Zoe wanted to stop and run through the fields, to enjoy their fragrance and beauty, but knew she had to keep moving. The more miles put between her and Runden Forest, all the better. A chill swept over her as she thought of Crendor. He was so angry that he would very likely come after her.

Suddenly she felt his presence, the same foul sense that she had in the cave. She spun around, looking in all directions. Nothing. It must have been her imagination running wild again.

When they stopped for a noontime meal, she saw a grove of apple trees beside the path near a lake. She walked Dapple to the lake to get some water and tied her to an apple tree so she could graze. When Zoe sat down with the basket of food, Brogan was right by her side. "Let's see what we have to eat, Brogan." She pulled out of the basket, boiled eggs, freshly baked bread, cheese, and grapes. When they were comfortably full, she put the remaining food back into the basket and picked some apples for later.

She did not realize how tired she was until she leaned her head against the tree. She fell asleep quickly and awoke to the late afternoon sun. "Oh my, Brogan. We need to go!"

Zoe hurriedly packed everything and climbed on Dapple. They had not traveled far when she saw a huge bird—it was Evan. He swooped down and landed.

"Zoe, you're in grave danger. Crendor and his whole tribe of triblens are less than a mile behind you. Quick, follow me—I know of a hidden cave not far from here. Crendor will not be able to find you there, at least not easily. Hurry, I must inform Arden about Crendor."

As they approached the cave, Zoe was wondering if maybe it would be better for her to ride on to the desert, but decided to trust Evan. When they were inside, Evan said, "You must get some brush and cover this entrance. This cave has been used by many of the King's followers as a haven. Stay here until Arden or I come." And with those words he flew away.

Zoe rushed to find some brush to cover the entrance. She comforted Brogan and Dapple, and then sat down to wait inside.

⋆═◉　✳　◉═⋆

Arden was on his way as soon as he could gather his friends. He thought Crendor would follow Zoe, but not this soon. He prayed to reach her in time. It was getting dark but that did not stop Arden. Fortunately, there was a full moon that helped to light the way. Evan flew back to find Crendor's location and then reported to Arden.

Evan quickly returned and proceeded to tell his news. "They are only about a quarter of a mile from Zoe right now."

Arden rubbed his chin, thinking. "That's too close. How far are we from them now?"

"About a mile."

"All right elves—this is the plan. We'll follow Evan and leave our horses as close as we can to the triblens. We must use wisdom if Zoe is to come out of this unharmed. Crendor is not aware of the cave, but he has a keen sense of smell, and will find her eventually. I didn't want it to come down to this, and I will first try to reason with Crendor, but if that doesn't work then we'll have to fight. Don't begin the fight until my signal. Is everything clear?" They all nodded in agreement. "Let's go then."

They had just tied their horses when Evan informed them that Crendor was within two hundred feet of the cave. They ran as fast as they could and hid behind some rocks. Arden shot an arrow in the tree, purposely and narrowly missing Crendor.

Crendor shouted. "Who goes there?" He knew the elves would not miss him unless they wanted to.

Arden stood up. "Crendor, you're violating your sentence by leaving Runden Forest. Go back or you will face the judgment."

Crendor smirked at his comment. "Who's going to bring me to judgment? You? I'm not worried about that. If you don't go back to the forest you'll face my judgment! But we don't have to fight. All I want is the girl. I know she is here somewhere for I have picked up her scent."

"You'll never get her, Crendor. She has been called by the King Himself."

A rage came over Crendor as he jerked his sword from its sheath. "The King! You're a fool for believing Him! He has long ago forgotten you. All who believe the fairy tale about a *journey* to Remiah become food for us. Prepare to fight!"

Arden counted fifteen triblens to twenty-three of them. He raised his sword and motioned to his warriors, "Fight in the name of the King!"

Immediately, Arden and his men ran forward to face the triblens. The elves were skilled swordsmen and archers, but the triblens had a considerable size advantage.

Crendor yelled, "This is for the death of Futney!" as he thrust his sword into the shoulder of Fergus, Arden's best friend. Arden was quickly by his side, blocking further blows from Crendor while dragging his friend behind a rock. The elves and triblens fought for over an hour with neither gaining the advantage. Finally, Crendor and Arden faced each other. They battled furiously, but soon, because of his massive size, Crendor began to tire. Arden fought with great energy, but even more with great wisdom, waiting patiently for his chance. When his chance came, he did not hesitate, but thrust his sword into Crendor's side. The huge beast staggered, and then fell to the ground. He tried to get up but his wound was deep and he soon lapsed unconscious.

When the triblens saw their leader was severely injured, they retreated into the forest, dragging him with them. Arden found Fergus and was glad to discover his wound was superficial—he would easily recover. He then checked on his other friends. Three elves were dead and several others were wounded. Grief started to sweep over Arden, when without warning Crendor reappeared enraged, running at him like a rabid dog. As Arden stood and lifted his sword, ready to fight, the rage in Crendor's face turned to terror. He staggered from his injury, and that was all Arden needed. Arden thrust his sword straight into Crendor's heart, instantly causing a fatal blow. Crendor fell to the earth with a crash.

Looking again, Arden saw that nine triblens were dead, including Crendor. He turned to Lorcan, his aid, and instructed him to see to the wounded. They carefully prepared the bodies of the dead elves for return to their families.

"I must go to Zoe, Evan. Please escort the others home and if there is any trouble, alert me, but I feel sure it will be a peaceful ride home. I don't believe the triblens will have the courage to attack us again for a long time, which is one good thing that has come from this battle.

"As you wish, my friend. I will escort the elves back and then return if needed." Hesitating, he circled for a minute, "I know you feel the loss of your friends, but they died with honor. You have won a great victory today. It may even result in good for the triblens. Now that their leader is dead maybe the rest will come to their senses."

"I hope you're right Evan. They are a pitiful lot, even though they are extremely dangerous. The King doesn't intend for any of His creatures to live the way they do. It is better to die fighting for the King than to live fighting for the evil one."

✳

"Dapple, it's going to be fine," Zoe said while trying to comfort her. She was getting restless waiting in the cave for so long. She patted Dapple for a long time. Soon everyone was tired and they settled down to sleep for the night.

Zoe awoke to the sound of her name being called. "Zoe, it's Arden. Wake up."

She recognized his voice immediately. "Arden, it really is you. I thought I was dreaming." He pulled her into his arms and held her close for a long time.

"Crendor is dead."

Zoe looked inquisitively at Arden. "What happened?"

We had a battle with the triblens not very far from here. I'm surprised you didn't hear us."

"I did hear the fighting, and I almost went to help."

Arden grinned. "I'm very glad you stayed here, Zoe!"

He put his hands on her shoulders. "You will be much safer now that Crendor is gone. Evan will continue to vigilantly watch over you and alert me to any further impending danger. As hard as it is for me to let you go, you must continue on your journey tomorrow—it will truly be the highlight of your life."

Zoe laughed. "I thought you were going to say that you were the highlight of my life!"

Arden smiled. "I do hope to be a highlight in your life, but I could never take the place of the King. You will understand this more once you are in Remiah. The keys you receive are foundational for your life's purpose. They not only reveal His nature, but also who you are called to be. As you continue the journey you'll find all of the keys to who you really are. Then the love that is just beginning between us will also grow."

Arden lifted her chin so that he could see her eyes. "Does this make sense to you?"

"Yes, I think so."

"Zoe, I know we are meant to be together. I love and care for you so much already that I can hardly bear the thought of being away from you."

"I care deeply for you too, Arden."

He smiled and took her in his arms. He gazed deeply into her beautiful eyes. He longed to kiss her but felt he should wait out of love and respect for her.

He held her for a long time finally breaking the silence. "It's only midnight, Zoe. I'm going to sleep outside the cave tonight and will leave after we have visited in the morning. I don't think the triblens will return now with Crendor dead, but I will feel better staying here tonight. Is this agreeable with you?"

"I would be most grateful." She leaned forward and kissed him on the cheek. She then went back into the cave to try to get some sleep.

Arden stood staring at where she had stood long after she had gone into the cave. As Evan had said so intuitively, it would take faith and patience for them to finally be together and share the love that he knew was destined for them. His patience was already being tried— he could hardly wait until the end of her journey so he could be with her at last. But then he thought, *she is definitely worth the wait.*

Believing and expecting with hope is faith.

Chapter Fourteen

Heed the sound of my cry for help, my King
and my God, for to Thee do I pray.
Psalm 5:2

The next morning Arden and Zoe talked for a long time about many things on their hearts. Too quickly the time came for Zoe to leave Arden and to once again travel on her chosen path.

Arden took her hands in his and kissed them. "Dunrow Desert is one of the most difficult parts of your journey. You will need to rest often and drink plenty of water. Will you remember this?"

"I will Arden, but you must not worry about me. Like you said, since the King has called me on this journey, He will take care of me."

"You are right of course." He patted Dapple on the head. "How do you like Dapple?"

"Oh, Arden, she is the finest horse I have ever ridden. She is sweet spirited, and very submissive to my commands. Thank you so much. I know she'll make my time in Dunrow Desert much easier."

"Dapple is a rare breed—her mother, Criosa, was my mother's favorite horse. It is only fitting that you should have Dapple."

Zoe blushed. "I must go, Arden. Twice you have come to my rescue—I am indebted to you."

He said the words that he thought so often. "It is my honor and my pleasure. I am at your service and my prayers will be with you, Zoe. I look forward to the day we shall be together at last."

"Oh Arden, please, we must wait until after the journey to speak of such things. We do not know what the future holds."

With great surety in his eyes, he replied, "But I do know, Zoe."

"Well, I need to know too, Arden. I enjoy your company, but I must know in my heart that we are meant to be together. If you believe this so greatly, pray that I will see it too. As wonderful as you are to me, I only want what the King wants in my life—that is all the promise I can give you right now."

"I understand how you feel Zoe, but my heart remains true and I will wait as long as it takes for you to see our future together too."

He then gave her a long embrace before reluctantly letting her go. Zoe climbed on Dapple and waved goodbye as she galloped on to her destination of Dunrow Desert and beyond.

When Zoe looked around, she could not have been more disappointed. The land looked like death. The heat from the sun and sand was so intense that she could hardly breathe. Dapple was maintaining an excellent pace, but Brogan was panting severely from the heat. She longed to go back to the beautiful forest with Arden, where there was so much shade that the sun could hardly be seen. *Oh, to sit under one of those trees with Arden would be heaven! Maybe this desert will not last too much longer,* she thought. But she was wrong. Even though they had walked several miles, the land was still flat and she could see nothing ahead of them but dry land—no trees or bushes anywhere. She looked at Brogan again and he was now dragging his feet. "Somehow we'll get through this Brogan."

The searing heat was burning Zoe's face as she felt the sweat trickle down her neck and back. The cloudless sky guaranteed there would be no rain for relief. She hurried the pace thinking there might be some shade up ahead. It only made matters worse because they were even hotter from the exertion. Her dress was clinging to her like a second skin. Soon even Dapple was beginning to show signs of fatigue, while she and Brogan became more and more weakened.

⊶ ✳ ⊷

Arden sat beneath the shade of a willow tree thinking about Zoe. How was she faring in Dunrow Desert? Was she remembering to drink enough water? He gave his worries to the King and was finally relieved.

After several days Evan flew to Runden Forest to talk to Arden. Arden saw him land and ran to him, "Hello, my friend. What news do you bring?"

"Zoe, Dapple, and Brogan are about a fourth of the way through Dunrow Desert. She has been traveling more than a week, and several times she nearly turned around. She is discouraged, but you must not go to her Arden. She must work through this herself. You know from what happened to you, that you walked around the desert three or four times before you stopped complaining and resolved to walk in patience. You would never have been the wise leader you are today without that experience. She has her own issues that the desert is meant to help her with. It will not help if you go to her now. The desert will make her stronger, and she will find her way out when she determines to submit to the King and trust that the desert is for her own good."

"You are right of course, Evan. I just wish she didn't have to go through that dreadful place."

"I submit to you Arden, that you should be happy she is going through that desert. She will be changed into a new and better woman once she gets through."

"Again, you have said the truth my friend."

"Well, I must go. I will keep you informed of Zoe's progress, as I am able.

"Thank you, Evan—a better friend there never was. A safe journey to you!"

⊶ ✳ ⊷

The desert sun continued to beat down relentlessly upon Zoe, Dapple, and Brogan until they were nearly delirious. Then, out of nowhere, tiny gnats appeared. They swarmed all around, burrowing into Zoe's flesh causing her to scream in pain. Brogan barked ferociously, snapping his jaws at the tiny creatures, but there were too many of them.

Zoe could see big, swollen welts on her arms and feel them on her face. They itched so badly that as she vigorously scratched them, they began to bleed, causing more bugs to bite her. Disheartened, she realized the flesh crawling bugs were poisonous. She could feel the poison sensation slowly spread through her whole body, and soon she began to feel nauseated. She called Brogan.

"We have to escape these creatures. Run!" But they could not keep up the pace because Zoe was so nauseated, and they had to slow down.

"It's of no use, Brogan. There are just too many. We cannot win against them!" Zoe fell off Dapple and sank down on the ground in surrender. She lay there for what seemed like hours, while the gnats preyed upon them. Surprisingly, anger welled up from deep inside, and she began swatting the bugs with a strength she did not know she possessed. Even so, it was a losing battle. There were just too many of them to kill. Finally she fell again to the ground in frustration and defeat.

"Who can win against so many horrible little creatures?" she muttered.

Then she yelled to the King, "You said to call on You when I needed help—I need help…" Her voice broke in sobs. "I…I do not know what to do…please help me." Brogan slunk down and nuzzled against her as if he were trying to shield her from more bites.

Then to her utter astonishment, a miracle occured—out of nowhere a strong wind came and blew all the bugs away. Zoe sat up and looked around in amazement. "They're gone!" Brogan's tail wagged wildly. "He really did hear us!"

Zoe lifted the small crystal bottle of water from her bag and gave some to Dapple and Brogan to drink. Then she drank some herself finding new refreshment with every swallow. It was still amazing to her that the water never stopped flowing from the bottle. She examined her bites and found many were still bleeding. Although she knew the ointment would heal them, she still felt like she needed to save it in case there were more serious injuries. So she decided to just cleanse the bites with water, and they all felt much better—even her stomach stopped hurting. She reached into her bag and looked at their food supply. They were down to just a few wafers and some apples, so they ate as little as they could to conserve the food.

Knowing that the King could hear her even in the desert gave Zoe new strength to continue the journey. They began a daily routine of waking up early and walking until midday. She made a small tent from her blanket to shield her from the sun, rested until it was cooler, and then they walked until dark. She found they could cover more distance with this routine. Only once did they find a bush to sleep under during the night. The other times they just slept under the stars.

Though they ate as little as absolutely necessary to survive and give them strength, after two weeks their food was finally gone. Still they pressed on. The pace slowed as they weakened, but they did not stop. After a couple of days Zoe knelt down to examine Brogan, and discovered that she could feel his ribs.

"I am so sorry Brogan—I wish I had some food for you." She lovingly patted him on the head and pulled him close to her. She loved Brogan more with each passing day. He not only protected her but he was a devoted friend. Her gaze turned to Dapple, grateful that she had her. She seemed to be doing fair, but she was showing signs of fatigue, too. But, at least they had water.

By the next day they were even more weak. After several weeks of enduring the desert and now without food, doubts began to swarm over Zoe as the bugs had earlier. *Why did I go on this journey…only to die in the desert?* After another day of no food, discouragement overcame Zoe and she said, "I've had enough. I can't do this any longer!"

She grumbled with every step she took, which only fed her discouragement. "I cannot believe I went on this journey. I should have known it would not work out." Zoe kicked the sand angrily. "I'm just a seamstress. How stupid of me to think that I could make it to the King's city. And to have a Prince fall in love with me! That had to be a joke, a mockery!"

Brogan looked up at her and when his eyes met hers, his ears went back and he hung his head low. Something about the way he looked at her turned Zoe's anger into sorrow. "I'm so sorry I put you through this." She knelt down and hugged him.

Zoe was carrying a weight, one that became heavier the more she complained. She sat down in the sand just staring—not knowing what to do. Brogan put his head on her lap. The sun fell past the horizon and with it fell her hopes of finishing the journey. She laid her head down in the sand, not even caring to pull out her mat to sleep on. During the night she woke with a start. She felt cold and then realized Brogan was not beside her anymore. She called him, but he did not come. She whistled, but he was nowhere in sight. She saddled Dapple and spent the rest of the night looking for Brogan, crying most of the time, feeling that he was gone forever. Never had she felt so hopeless. Never had she felt so defeated. She slid off of Dapple onto the ground, falling to her knees, and doing what she should have done so very long ago.

He will answer when we call—every time!

Chapter Fifteen

"For ye have need of patience, that, after ye have done
the will of God, ye might receive the promise."
Hebrews 10:36 (KJV)

Zoe begged for the King to help her. "Please, I know I've complained about this journey and I'm so sorry. But please… please bring Brogan back to me," she sobbed.

Zoe rode Dapple back to where she left her things and began searching and calling for Brogan again, but he did not come. It was almost midday and she was just about to give up, when she heard a bark. She turned around and saw Brogan running toward her. She hopped off Dapple and ran as fast as she could to meet him.

"Oh, Brogan…you're back! I am so ashamed of my behavior and I'm so sorry." She could see he had something in his mouth. "What is it fella?"

"You found a pear! Is that where you were—looking for food?" He ran ahead and Zoe followed. Soon they stood beside a huge pear tree, right in the desert. She ate one and immediately felt better. "I don't think I've ever tasted anything so good. Thank you Brogan!" Zoe picked as many pears as she could carry and took them to Dapple, who gladly ate them all. Brogan was so happy that he kept bringing Zoe pears to throw and retrieve.

Zoe was amazed that Brogan was happily munching on a pear. "I didn't know you liked pears Brogan—I guess anything would taste good now!" She grabbed him and held him close.

When it was time to rest for the night, they slept peacefully under the full moon. As they awoke in the morning, Zoe decided the best thing to do would be to stop complaining about the desert.

It certainly had not helped in the past—it only made her dwell on how bad everything looked.

They ate more pears, packed as many as Dapple's saddlebags could hold, and once again began their journey. Zoe was so thankful Brogan was back with her that she even felt cheerful. As she watched him, she realized that he was full-grown and what a fine wolf he had become. Sometimes when she talked to Brogan, he looked as if he could understand everything she said. *Maybe he does,* she thought.

Later in the day Zoe could see a body of water in the distance. She quickly took out her map and looked. *It's the Crystal Sea! I must remember to look at the map more often!* "Come on Dapple and Brogan! Run!" They ran and ran, but they never could find the sea. Then Zoe realized she had just seen a mirage. She took out her map and looked again.

"The Crystal Sea is right here on the map Brogan. I don't understand. I suppose we'll just keep walking. Here, drink some water." Each of them drank until their thirst was quenched.

Though it was hot, Dapple had learned to go at a pace that did not exhaust her. They walked for several more miles through the barren land and then Zoe again saw what she thought was the sea. This time they did not run. But as they approached the sea, it did not disappear.

"We reached the Crystal Sea, Brogan! Come on, jump in!" Even Dapple waded into the water up to her chest.

There were no trees or grass that surrounded the sea, just white sand, but the water was cool and refreshing and was just as translucent blue as she had imagined it would be. Brogan jumped, splashed, and kept sticking his head underneath the water. Soon he was catching fish and putting them on shore. Zoe felt that they must be close to a forest because an abundance of driftwood had washed ashore and was dry. She made a fire to cook the fish, and then cleaned and cooked them. Soon they had a feast of fish and pears. Zoe was so full that she felt useless and decided to rest a little while.

When she awoke, she realized she had not taken the time to write in her journal lately, and there was so much to write about. She sat down by the sea and wrote about Brogan, and her thankfulness to have him. And Dapple, what a joy she was. Then her thoughts drifted to Arden. It was amazing to Zoe that he wanted to marry her. Could it really be possible? Was that their destiny? Zoe thought long and hard about this. She had very much wanted to marry and have a family, but to marry a real Prince, and one as wonderful as Arden, just seemed too good to be true. She had trouble giving her heart to him because of this.

Zoe wrote down what she was feeling about Arden, thinking that it might bring clarity to her feelings. She wrote about how he rescued her twice, how handsome, kind, and brave he was. He was affectionate and she had to admit that she was very attracted to him. More importantly, he had gone to Remiah and was a friend of the King. He really was everything she could possibly want in a husband, and much more. So, what was holding her back? Perhaps she did not know how to love in that way. She thought that maybe her love for people had grown cold over the years— perhaps from the rejection by her mother. Could that be it? But no, she loved Geneva and Feena. She cared for Arden, but was it the kind of love required for marriage? Maybe she just needed to get to know him better. She laid those thoughts aside, closed her journal, and then walked along the shoreline.

Brogan awoke from his nap and soon found her. He jumped in the water playfully, but before long his concentration turned to catching more fish. Zoe gathered wood, started a nice fire, and cleaned and cooked the many fish Brogan had caught. After they ate, she played in the water with him and then rode Dapple along the shoreline. This was so much better than the desert!

As much fun as it was by the Crystal Sea, after two days Zoe felt the need to press on. She took out the map and studied it. The road would take them away from the sea and through many more miles of desert. Dread came over Zoe as she looked at it. For a time she even considered just staying by the sea. They could live here and have plenty. But she knew they had to go on. They had made it this far so they could make it the rest of the way. Before leaving she decided to ponder the first part of their journey through the desert, what they had done wrong, and what they could do to make it easier. Finally she concluded that the only thing she could do to make it easier was not to complain and try to be thankful for even being chosen for such a journey. This she resolved to do.

Thus they started the journey again and walked until noon. "The fish will not keep very long in this heat, so we better go ahead and eat them first. We still have lots of pears left, but we'll probably have to find some food along the way. At least we have the King's water, so we will not go thirsty in this dry place." Zoe continued to talk to Brogan just like he could respond because some day she believed he would.

Days turned into weeks as they walked through the desert. The scenery never changed, and although they had traveled longer on this leg than on the first one—it seemed so much easier! Zoe could not understand what was different, but she had changed. The harder the walk in the desert became, the more determined she was to be thankful and cheerful. She was beginning to get stronger and started to even feel noble, maybe even like a Princess.

Brogan and Dapple even seemed to be having an easier time. She began to realize how her complaining had made things harder for everyone. She knew now that this desert had been good for her, to help her learn patience. She resolved to remain patient and thankful, regardless of what happened on the rest of the journey. She knew if she would stay on the path that she had been given, everything would be all right.

From the distance Zoe saw they were approaching a rock formation. Then she saw something glistening in the sun. She hopped off Dapple to see what it was. It was another key! She picked it up, and read the inscription—*PATIENCE*. Zoe felt like jumping up and down. "Oh, Brogan—another key! This is the third now." As she placed the key in her pocket, she knew now that patience was truly planted within her, and she prayed that it would continue to grow.

She jumped back on Dapple and stroked her long mane. Zoe felt very grateful to receive this key. She knew that this one was going to help her not only in the desert, but for the rest of the journey. She continued on her path with a new lightness of heart that even her companions shared.

The key to patience is the willingness to endure trials with thankfulness while trusting in the King—even in the driest of places.

Chapter Sixteen

*Watch the path of your feet, and all
your ways will be established.*
Proverbs 4:26

Something was wrong—Arden could feel it. Even though Evan had just returned and reported that Zoe was doing fine, something was amiss. She had passed the Crystal Sea and would soon leave the desert, but he could not let go of this unsettling feeling. Suddenly he knew—it was the triblens and he felt they were up to something very bad.

Arden's concern was obvious as Evan watched him approach. "What is it my friend?"

"Evan, I have been greatly troubled since I awoke this morning. I feel it has something to do with the triblens."

"When you are troubled there is usually a problem. I'll go and investigate."

"Thank you Evan—I really appreciate it."

"I will return as soon as I can."

Waiting for Evan proved to be a long time. Arden prayed to the King and asked Him to protect Zoe. He also prayed that the King would give him discernment over what was troubling him so greatly.

As Arden was deep in prayer, Evan finally returned. "Arden, you were right. We thought when Crendor died, they would not trouble us any longer—this is not the case. In fact, there is now even more danger. I flew to their territory and landed in a tree where they would not suspect my entry. I overhead Jarleth, their new leader talking to some other triblens. He wants revenge for Crendor and Futney, as well as the other triblens that were killed in that battle. I am sad to report that they are gathering many wicked creatures of the forest to track Zoe down and kill her. They also said that while they were at it they might as well get rid of as many of the King's followers as they could."

Arden was pacing the ground as Evan spoke. "As I was praying, the King told me to prepare for a battle. Which creatures is Jarleth gathering?" Evan hesitated. "Evan, I must know who we are up against."

"He has called all the triblens in the territory to mobilize. He has also enlisted the witches, warlocks, Kavian and his clan, and any other followers of Durgalt they can find. The gruelas have been called to spread fear throughout the land. I overhead Jarleth say they were going to wait a few weeks before they would fight. He said we would be off guard then, thinking that there was now peace between us."

Arden sat down when he heard the news. "This is going to be the biggest battle we have ever faced—all because of a single girl who just wants to reach the city of the King! She must have an awesome destiny, more so than I considered. My wanting her to be my Princess may have blinded me to something even greater that she is called to do. She must have a great purpose with the King, so we must protect her at all costs! We must also protect our people and our friends from this evil horde that is gathering.

"We had best start planning how to win this battle. It is not enough to just defeat them. That is what we did in the last battle and it has only created a greater threat. We only have a few weeks to prepare, and you know how they change their minds frequently. We must get ready for this battle immediately. I must contact my father. I'm going to need your help, Evan—I'm going to need you a lot."

"I understand, and you know that I'm at your service Arden. Just tell me what to do."

"Father is helping a friend, King Bevin, who is leader of another group of elves in Vargo Valley. Bevin is recuperating from an injury he suffered during a battle with Hasten, the warlock.

Father is administering his dominion until he recovers. Do you know where Vargo Valley is located?"

"Yes, I know where it is."

"Good. Once you find my father, ask him to gather all the elves and followers of the King that he can find. We are going to need all of the help we can get. Then go to Feena, Antrum, Bantry, and the rest of the King's followers in Hemlock Forest and see if they can join us. They are skilled in fighting. I will gather all of our friends in this area too. There are also the malios and fregors. Since they are farther north, and Zoe is traveling toward them, it would be best if they stayed where they are. Our rendezvous point will be where they live—the land of Ferlan. I feel this is where the battle will take place. One other thing—ask them to bring all of their weapons. If we lose this battle, there may not be another one."

"I will be glad to help, but I must ask you one thing. Should King Ronan not lead King Bevin's army while you lead his?"

"That is a good question my friend, but we need him here. His friend will revive much faster when he learns of the impending battle. They are great warriors. My father may already know he needs to get home. He discerns so many things about the future."

"Another thing, Evan. I am not sure of Zoe's location now. Could you find out exactly where she is? She must continue on her journey for now, and she may not have time to escape the traps that delay so many when they are close to coming out of the wilderness. After you have told the others of the impending battle, you will need to find her and keep me informed of her precise location, as well as any problems that she is having. It is my hope that within one week she will have made it to Ferlan. If she avoids any major traps she should also arrive there at about the same time that we do. If not, we will have to find her.

"Evan, I do not want you to tell Zoe about this battle yet. She may needlessly worry when there is nothing she can do about it at this time. If possible, don't even let her see you. Just check on her location and return to me with details. Thank you so much Evan. Your help has been invaluable and will continue to be. You are the best of friends."

"Thank you, Arden. And I will say that this is a very good plan. I will do my best to find everyone and return as soon as I can with all the information I am able to secure." With those words Evan flew away to begin the great mobilization.

Arden went to his favorite place to pray—his house in the trees. There he could think clearly and seek the King for wisdom and strategy.

Brogan's tail was wagging with such force that it was beginning to hurt Zoe's legs. "Why are you so happy this morning?" She scratched his head and ears. "Are you hungry? Well, let's eat some breakfast then. We only have pears, but at least we have food."

Although it was not entirely satisfying, the fruit gave them the strength to continue. Zoe played with Brogan for a while, and then walked over to Dapple and spoke soothing words to her. Then once again they began walking on the path where the desert seemed to never end.

When night came, Zoe took out her journal and wrote under candlelight about this difficult part of her journey. It was hot and tiring, but there was still much to be thankful for. The King was teaching her many things. So far she had received three keys: *PEACE, FAITHFULNESS,* and *PATIENCE.* She wondered how many more keys there were. At any rate, she knew she needed to keep pushing forward and abide in the King's peace even in Dunrow Desert.

Brogan laid his head on her lap and was soon fast asleep. He certainly was a faithful friend and so was Dapple. Her thoughts abruptly drifted toward Arden. She wondered what he was doing. She thought about Crendor—she was sorry he died but the worry of him coming after her was gone now. And what about Kavian? Somehow she felt she had not seen the last of him. Though her mind was active, her body was tired. She soon fell asleep and found herself dreaming about a young man named Arden.

The night passed peacefully and to Zoe's delight, when she awoke, the weather had changed from the scorching heat to a more refreshing temperature. She realized she had been on this journey nearly six months now—it would soon be autumn. Somehow it seemed to have been both much longer and much shorter than six months. Many things had happened in that time. Her life had become a true adventure—just like those she once believed could only be found in fairy tales.

As they walked farther that day, the barren desert became scattered with little green shoots of grass, and small trees growing in the distance. Zoe could not have been happier. She had passed the test and was truly leaving the desert. The grass began to get thicker and flowers appeared. Beautiful pink, yellow, and purple pansies shone in the sun like rainbows of colored glass. Zoe took out her map and discovered they were in Linder Valley.

As they continued on, a burst of color from the trees and flowers brought new hope and joy to Zoe. Where there had been no growth in the desert, vegetation was now lush and fertile. Autumn leaves in reds, browns, and yellows swirled around her feet. The wind was cooler so she pulled out the cape that Feena had given her and pulled it over her shoulders, immediately feeling warmer.

The beauty of the valley was breathtaking at times. They walked through a field of red poppies that swayed in the cool, gentle breeze. As they followed the path, they could hear a gurgling stream flowing over rocks. It brought back many memories of the stream that she used to love sitting by in front of her house. The little stream grew wider and then it began to connect with other streams along the way until it formed a river. She took out her map and discovered it was the Cashel River. Fish were swimming everywhere in the water, which suddenly made Zoe very hungry.

"Look, Brogan! Are you ready to catch some more fish?" While Dapple grazed on the lush grasses of fall, Zoe motioned for Brogan to jump in the water. He knew exactly what to do. He was back within ten minutes, and Zoe already had a nice fire going to cook the fish. Cleaning the fish took little time and soon they were ready to eat. Their mouths watered as the aroma tantilized their appetites. At last the fish were ready and they ate until they could eat no more. Sunset was approaching, so they decided to stay and make camp.

"It's so beautiful here Brogan, and hard to believe that just a few miles back we were in a desert. Just look around—take in the loveliness." She tenderly looked at Brogan and dreamed that one day he would answer her.

Meanwhile in Runden Forest, Evan returned. "Well, my friend, did you find Zoe?"

"Yes, she is in Linder Valley and doing quite well."

"That is good news. She is making excellent progress. What of my father? Did you find him?"

"Yes, and as you thought, he was already planning his return. King Bevin is almost completely healed now, and he, too, is anxious to assist in the battle. His people have grown tired of the harassment from their enemies, and they all want to wage war to regain peace in their land. At this time he is gathering all of the King's followers in the surrounding areas as well. Word will travel quickly and I expect within three days they will all be here."

"Thank you Evan. You have been invaluable! What about Feena, Bantry, Antrum, and the others?"

"I have contacted them all—even the malios and fregors. Feena, Bantry, and Antrum will arrive within two days by the Cashel River. The malios and fregors will search for Zoe and inform her of our impending plan."

Arden rubbed his chin as if in deep thought. "Our plan must be flexible for Zoe's sake. I will have to ask you to keep a close watch on her whereabouts so we can make any necessary adjustments. You know the lay of the land better than anyone. I have given great thought and prayer to our strategy. Choosing the ground on which we fight is crucial. I know we don't have time to go through the desert. I believe it would be best to travel by the Cashel River—it will be the quickest way for us to arrive in Ferlan. What do you think Evan?"

"It is a good strategy. The path that Zoe is traveling runs next to the river for quite a distance. We may even find her that way."

"Good. It is time to gather our people and have them make ready their weapons. We don't know how many of Durgalt's followers we will be fighting. For this battle we will need all of our resources."

"That is wise, Arden. If you would like, I will carry your command to the others."

"Yes, do it. We can no longer hold anything back. This time our enemies will not hold anything back.

Evan hesitated, "Arden, this will be the great war that has been prophesied for many years. Many had even begun to think that it would never come, but now it is upon us."

Arden's eyes widened. "As you spoke, I felt in my heart that this is true. At last, we will fight the war that we have been waiting for. We can win Evan—we have to!

⚬⟹ ✳ ⟸⚬

Zoe, Dapple, and Brogan continued on the straight path but it soon began to curve. In the distance there was a beautiful little stone cottage with a thatched roof. How pleasant and quaint it looked in the midst of the lush green grass and flowers. There was a well-tended vegetable garden beside the cottage. Though the weather was cooler, the garden still had plenty of fresh vegetables available. She was curious as to who lived in such a grand little place, so she knocked on the door and to her surprise Kieran, the King's messenger, answered.

"How good to see you again Zoe, and you too Brogan. Oh, I see you have a new friend."

"Yes, her name is Dapple." Zoe still could not believe Kieran answered the door. "My goodness, is this where you live?"

"Oh no. The King sent me here to prepare the cottage for you. There is a fierce storm coming and He wants you to stay here until it is over."

"How wonderful to have shelter!" Zoe's brow furrowed. "What kind of storm do you mean?"

"Oh, nothing you should worry about. You will be safe here. Let me show you around. The fireplace is ready to be lit, and the food is already laid out on the table for you to enjoy. There is plenty more food in the pantry, and freshly baked bread from the King's kitchen. He sent some fresh cheese from His dairy and vegetables from His own garden. As you can see, there are still some vegetables in the fall garden outside. Make yourself at home and stay here until the storm is over. You will be just fine. There is a barn behind the dogwood trees for Dapple to stay during the storm. Now that you are here I must be going. I have much business to attend to for the King. There is a great stirring I sense."

"Thank you so much Kieran, and please send our sincerest gratitude to the King for this unexpected and welcome provision."

"I will tell Him, but remember you can tell Him also. I will see you again soon." Kieran patted Brogan on the head and then left.

Zoe lit the logs and before long there was a blazing fire in the open fireplace. Zoe's eyes wandered to the quilt covered bed in the corner. *Oh to sleep in a nice warm bed!*

Zoe walked to the table where the cheese and bread looked so appetizing. She ate some and savored each delicious mouthful. She also shared it with Brogan. She wanted to prepare a nice supper for them so she tried not to eat too much. She went outside and picked some carrots and gave them to Dapple, and in turn Dapple neighed in delight. "You have been such a good girl on this trip, and you have become a special friend too." After Dapple ate, Zoe walked her to the barn. There was hay in a stall and oats that Dapple immediately began eating. "I'll check on you later girl. Enjoy your dinner—you deserve it!"

Thinking about the vegetables, Zoe decided to make vegetable stew just like Feena used to make. The preparations did not take long and soon it was ready. When she sat down to eat, she gave thanks to the King for this little haven and their nice hot meal.

Zoe smiled as she watched Brogan clean his plate. After she washed the dishes, she sat by the fireplace enjoying the comfort of a cozy home. Brogan curled up beside her feet and went to sleep. She too was soon lulled to sleep by the gentle sound of the embers crackling in the fire.

Then Brogan's ears picked up something. His eyes opened and he sat up, watching the door. He looked over at his young master as she slept soundly. All was right in their little world, but still something was stirring far away that he could feel. He settled down again, closed his eyes, and entered a deep sleep that was rare for his kind.

Perfect peace comes to those who
totally trust in Him.

Chapter Seventeen

And everyone who competes in the
games exercises self-control in all things.
I Corinthians 9:25

Kieran had been right about the storm. The little cottage became a haven for Zoe and Brogan as the winds raged and the cold rain poured down all that day and night, until the next morning. Thankfully, it gave them time to catch up on some much needed rest. Zoe also took the time to write in her journal as Brogan lazily enjoyed the luxury of sleeping in front of a nice warm fire.

When the rain finally stopped, she and Brogan went outside to feel the warmth of the sun and breathe in the clean smell. They could hear Dapple neighing in the barn, so Zoe let her out to enjoy the fresh air.

They spent the rest of the day relaxing in the beautiful garden and taking a long nap in the afternoon. The next morning they packed some extra food, closed the door behind them, and once again began their walk on the chosen path.

❋

At the same time Zoe was beginning her journey again, Prince Arden, King Ronan, and King Bevin were gathering elves and all of the King's followers who were willing to wage war against Jarleth and the evil creatures who served Durgalt. So far they had gathered a group numbering more than three hundred, with each one confident in their cause—ready to fight for justice in the name of the King. Feena, Bantry, and Antrum and many others from

Hemlock Forest were on their way and would soon arrive in Runden Forest.

But there was one who had already arrived who no one was expecting to see. He was the wisest prophet known in the King's territory, as well as the oldest. He had not been seen in two years, so when Arden saw him he ran to his old friend.

"At long last, Mahon, you have returned to Runden Forest! We are honored to have you join us."

Mahon shook Arden's hand heartily. "Arden, my boy—it's good to see you too. I am here for a purpose though." His deep blue eyes shone with intensity. "The time has finally come. I have foreseen this war for many years."

Arden could not hide his concern. "What do you know of this war, Mahon?"

"With every passing moment the enemy is gathering more and more of his vile followers." As if he knew Arden's mind, he said, "You had but one thought—to save Zoe, but this war involves far more than saving your beloved. It is a war against evil—light against darkness."

"I have felt that this impending war is the one."

"Your vision is growing more clear because you are growing in wisdom and understanding of the King's ways. By seeking Him, you will find the truth, for He is the One who gives light to our vision."

Arden could not help but notice the light that shone from Mahon's face. His eyes revealed a man who had suffered in life yet prevailed. His long hair and beard were almost pure white, not only revealing that he had lived long, but also representing purity in his wisdom. He spoke sparingly, but each word had significant meaning. Arden felt like he could learn much from this man.

"Will you help us, Mahon?"

"I have come for no other purpose. You are gathering friends from the North; I have called the King's followers from the South."

Arden was puzzled. "How far south?"

"South of Brenlough there are many who serve the King faithfully in the land of Parthalon."

"I had no idea of this. I always thought that land was barren except for a few hideous creatures that always stayed to themselves."

"Ah, but appearances can be deceiving my friend. Yes, they do look different, but the Parthalonians have hearts of gold. I have been living in their land for the past two years and have gained a wealth of knowledge from them." Mahon looked toward a huge cave behind the bushes where his friend was standing. "Come Keely, and meet my friend, Arden."

Arden could only stare. The creature was humped over like an old man and covered with gray fur. He was no more than four feet tall with arms that reached almost to his feet. His eyes bulged from a head that was too large for his body, while his rounded ears stood straight up on his head. He walked with a slight limp as he approached.

"Arden, I am pleased to introduce you to Keely, leader of the Parthalonians. I have great admiration for him and stand amazed at his courage and brilliance. He has also brought one hundred of his people who have the same unwavering focus and will be a great asset in our war."

Arden bowed. "I am very pleased to meet you Keely, and thank you for bringing your people."

Keely was most gracious as he bowed in return. "I have heard much about you from Mahon and am honored to finally make your acquaintance. We have gathered here to fight against the wicked slaves of Durgalt so that the King's peace may once again reign in our land."

Arden's brow furrowed. "I had no idea that our enemies were harassing you."

"Yes, we have had our share of battles. "

Arden felt admiration for Keely and all the Parthalonians. "You have come a great distance and joined forces with us against our enemies—for this I am grateful. But Zoe will soon be in grave danger. We must save her and rally together to fight our enemies."

Mahon focused intently on Arden. "I understand your concern for Zoe, but she is a strong warrior and will be of great benefit in this war."

"How do you know Zoe, Mahon? She is young—only eighteen."

Mahon just smiled. "Arden, she is much stronger than you know. She is a skilled archer, focused, and determined—strong assets for anyone in battle. Look at Keely. He is not large in stature, yet his archery skills are unrivaled. Indeed, he is the same man who once saved Feena's life and taught her the archery skills that she now possesses. He serves no other than the King and therefore his vision is clear."

"I see what you are saying, but I believe Zoe is to be my bride. How can I let her fight, knowing that there is a great possibility she may not survive the battle?"

With compassion Mahon said, "You must trust the King with Zoe. He will give you the peace that will enable you to let go of her so she can fulfill her destiny. Can you do this?"

Arden looked down at the ground. "I know I must."

"Good. This war grows closer with every passing minute. Let us now take council so when the others arrive in Ferlan we may share our plan of attack. They too will come with a war plan. We will put these parts together and complete our strategy. We must leave for Ferlan before nightfall, so come, let us begin our battle plan."

→▭ ✳ ▭←

Zoe felt an urgency to keep moving forward. A forceful gust of wind picked up and suddenly the air turned cold. The farther they walked, the colder it became. Zoe put on her cape, and pulled it tight around her neck. *I am so thankful Feena gave me this cape,* she thought. They walked for several hours facing the brisk wind while the temperature continued to plummet.

"Brogan, we need to find shelter soon. Otherwise, we'll have to turn around and go back to the cottage. With these clouds getting thicker and the temperature dropping, unbelievable as it seems, it could snow." Soon their joints became infected with the cold. But thankfully they spotted a small cottage up ahead.

"Look! Maybe these people will let us spend the night."

Zoe knocked on the door and a small elderly woman appeared. "Well, bless your souls, you poor dears—you're almost frozen!" She nearly bowled them over pulling them inside.

A welcome fire was burning and the aroma of freshly baked bread tantalized their appetites. "What are you doing in the middle of nowhere on a day like today? You should know better," she scolded in a motherly tone.

"We're on a journey," Zoe replied. "We didn't know the weather would be turning so cold, or we would have stayed where we were for a few more days."

The woman looked at Zoe with questioning eyes. "What is your name?"

"I am Zoe Newbridge and this is Brogan. Dapple my horse, is tied to the tree outside."

"Mighty fine looking wolf you have there. I bet he is good protection for you. We'll go put your horse in the barn." They walked to the barn as snowflakes began to swirl all around them. They fed Dapple some hay, closed the door tightly, and walked back to the little cottage.

"Thank you and—"

"You just did get here in time," the old woman interrupted. "Now take your cape off and come sit by the fire. You can call me Nanny. Are you hungry? I just baked some bread and I was fixin' to sit down and eat some vegetables with it. Come and join me. We'll eat and talk at the same time. I have been mighty lonely since my husband passed away last year. Oh, I miss him. We would talk for hours mostly about nothing really. He could even out talk me! He was a fine carpenter. Oh, I forgot—we haven't said the blessing yet!"

"Our dear King, bless this food and bless Zoe, Brogan, and Dapple." She continued talking without even taking a breath. "As

I was saying, my Henry was a fine carpenter. He made every bit of the furniture you see in this room."

"It's beaut—" Zoe began.

"That hutch over there is made out of the finest oak in the land. He hand carved every bit of it."

"Oh, he must have been—" Zoe was trying not to get frustrated but she could not get a single sentence in.

"My Henry built this cottage too. Those stones in that fireplace were hand picked from the river and fit together in a special design. Do you see it?"

"Well…"

"Look closely now. There's a cross in the stones near the top."

"Oh, yes, I see it now."

"Here have some more vegetables. You need some meat on your bones. You're too thin! I love to eat and I guess it shows! I could eat a wheelbarrow full of potatoes in one sitting if my stomach would hold them!"

Nanny continued talking for hours. Zoe had never heard anyone talk so much in all her life. *Does she even breathe?*

Finally and thankfully, it was now dark and they could go to bed. "You two can sleep over there in the corner. There is a cot for you Zoe and a nice warm rug for Brogan. Now go on to sleep and get some rest."

"Thank you for the wonderful meal, and for allowing us to stay here. You're very kind."

"Oh, it's my pleasure. Goodnight my dear." She scratched Brogan behind the ears and then went to bed.

Zoe went to bed with her head throbbing. She looked outside the window and saw that it was still snowing. *Maybe it will stop snowing tonight and warm up tomorrow so we can leave*, she thought. But that was not to be—in the morning she awoke to an angry, howling wind with snowdrifts two feet tall, and it was still snowing heavily.

"Oh, you two are up. Come on over here and eat! I made scones and eggs. I also have some strawberry jam I made this summer.

Do you want some milk to drink? Well, sit down. It looks like you're going to have to stay here for a while, so we might as well enjoy ourselves."

All through the day and into the night Nanny continued to talk. "I was one of eight children, and I was the oldest so I was expected to do the most. Mama died giving birth to baby John when I was just twelve years old. I had to take over all the cooking, cleaning, and watching my seven brothers and sisters. I did just about everything while my father worked in the fields. It was a hard life. Father remarried when I was thirteen so my stepmother took over the cooking, but I still had to clean and watch the kids. And then father and my stepmother had three more kids. Can you imagine eleven kids in one house? Talk about noise! I thought I would go crazy when all those kids started fighting and wanting this and that. But I didn't have to watch them too long because I met my Henry and we got married when I was sixteen. We were married for fifty-five years before he died. Oh how I miss him. We had five children, but they don't live near me anymore so I am here all alone most of the time. They do visit occasionally."

If she said one more word, Zoe thought she would scream, but then Nanny stopped abruptly and said. "I'm going to bed. Goodnight, hope you sleep well."

They heard her lightly snoring in the bedroom. As Zoe lay in bed, she was so tense that she could not go to sleep for a long time. But finally she drifted off about midnight. When they awoke the next morning, Nanny was humming at the fireplace and frying bacon.

She must have seen Zoe out of the corner of her eye, because she began talking again. "Good morning. Are you hungry? I hope so. I've made lots of blueberry pancakes. I have some fresh maple syrup too. Go wash your hands, come on over here, and sit down before these pancakes get cold."

Zoe fixed a plate of pancakes and bacon for Brogan and set them on the floor. As she ate, she wondered if this was going to be another day of Nanny's nonstop talking. "These pancakes are delicious. Thank you. Oh, after breakfast, I need to go check on Dapple."

"Oh, no need. I've already been out, milked Tess, and fed them both. Dapple is as snug as can be. You know, I love to cook and without my Henry here, I haven't felt like cooking much. Henry was the kindest man you would ever meet. He helped anybody in need. He would cut wood and bring it to some of our neighbors who were disabled. Last year he was cutting down a tree for old Mrs. Bray, a widow, who lives about a mile from here. He came home after he delivered the wood and said he was feeling poorly and thought he would skip supper and lie down for a while. Well, I knew something was wrong then. Henry never turned down my cooking! I ate my meal alone and then I went to check on him, but he was already gone. I did not even get to say goodbye. It still hurts when I think about it," she confided. "But I know he is happy and in a good place. One day, I'll be with him again and I look forward to that day. Well enough about that. Since you've come, my old joy for cooking has come back to me. Have some more pancakes."

"No thank you—"

"Oh, come on now. There are five more sitting here for you."

"Well, all right, I'll eat one more."

"That's my girl. You know, this recipe is an old family secret. Those blueberries are from the bushes my Henry planted for me out back, and they are the best I've ever eaten. We'll not get anymore now for it is much too cold. But that is all right because I will have more next year. Every other year those blueberries are just falling off the bushes. I don't know what I'll do with all of them. You'll have to come back and visit so we can eat pancakes and muffins all summer long."

Nanny kept on talking all morning. Finally, Zoe interrupted her and said she really needed to check on Dapple. She stayed in the barn longer than she really should have. She was sure Nanny was expecting her to return quickly since it was so cold, but she just could not listen to her talk another minute.

"I envy you out here Dapple—it's so nice and peaceful." Zoe gave Dapple some more hay and since she knew Nanny would come and get her anytime, she walked back inside.

"Oh there you are. I was getting ready to bundle up and go outside and check on you!"

She talked about her children for half the morning, and then Zoe just sat staring at her until her words began to stream together. She stood up and began to pace the floor while trying to hold her tongue, knowing that if she said anything she would regret it.

"Are you okay, Zoe? I know what it is. These four walls are closing in on you. I thought it would help you to get outside a little while, but I guess it didn't. You seemed jittery yesterday and again today. I know how that is. Last year I was stuck in this cottage for two weeks with a blizzard that was the worst I have seen in all my days. This one will probably melt quicker than that one because it's early for such a large snow. I know what we could do! We'll get some snow and make snow cream! My mother used to make that when I was a little girl and it was so good. She put a little honey in the snow, mixed it up real good, and then added some crushed vanilla bean and a little cream. We kids thought it was the best thing we had ever tasted except for the time—"

"Oh, please be quiet!" Zoe screamed.

She turned to face Nanny and saw the hurt in her eyes. Nanny stopped in mid-sentence, opened, and then closed her mouth. She shifted a little in her seat, and stared at the floor for what seemed like an hour to Zoe. Finally Nanny spoke.

"You're right, my Henry used to tell me the same thing, that I talked too much." A single tear fell down her cheek. "I've just been so lonely and it felt so good to have someone to talk with that I got carried away. I am so sorry."

Zoe stood up and went over and hugged Nanny. "I am the one who should be sorry, Nanny, not you. I was wrong to say that to you. Will you forgive me?"

"Why, yes of course. I understand. We'll just put it behind us."

There was an uncomfortable silence again for a few minutes, but then Nanny continued to talk, not quite as much though. The next day, Zoe really tried to listen to Nanny and discovered that she was just a sweet, lonely old woman who had no one to talk to.

They had been with Nanny for three days when the weather turned warm enough for the snow to begin melting. The next day Nanny asked, "You know I have talked so much that I don't even know where you're going."

Zoe smiled. "We're going to Remiah."

"How wonderful! I know the King myself. I met Him when I was ten years old. Henry was a follower of the King, too."

Zoe touched Nanny's arm. "When you become lonely, it would be a good time to talk to the King."

"Since Henry died, I've been talking to the King more than I ever did. But now that you mention it, I think I will just carry on conversations with Him all day."

That night when Zoe went to bed, she realized what a generous, loving, and caring woman Nanny really was. She had developed a special place in her heart for that kind, old woman, and actually found that she felt compassion for her and even enjoyed her stories. She looked at Brogan and he was already fast asleep. Zoe opened her journal and a key fell out. She picked it up and read the inscription: *SELF-CONTROL*. She knew she had learned much from Nanny about self-control, but she also knew she had a long way to go. But now that she had the key, it would begin to grow deep within. Without self-control, how could she ever follow the King to the fullest? He certainly had been patient with her. Now she must do the same with others. She placed the key in her pocket and felt the seed of self-control begin new life within her.

The key to self-control is having patience blended with kindness.

Chapter Eighteen

With all humility and gentleness, with patience,
showing forbearance to one another in love.
Ephesians 4:2

Now that most of the snow has melted, we have to leave today Nanny. But thank you so much for letting us stay with you. I'm going to miss you—I really mean that! I don't know what we would have done if you hadn't taken us in."

"You're welcome, Zoe. Come anytime, and I promise not to talk your ears off next time!"

They laughed, hugged, and said their goodbyes. Nanny handed them a huge bag of food for their journey.

"You are a sweet woman, Nanny. Thank you so much for your kindness." Zoe hugged her again. "May the King bless you and take care of you."

They waved goodbye and then once again were off on their journey to Remiah.

⊷⇒ ✳ ⇐⊶

They walked several miles down the road and then stopped abruptly. "What was that noise? Come on Brogan." Zoe climbed down quietly from Dapple and tied her to a tree.

They heard the noise again. Brogan sniffed the air, found the scent, and then tracked his way to some mulberry bushes. Zoe followed and gasped when she saw an animal's legs sticking out from underneath the bushes. She walked closer and examined the animal, only to nearly faint when she saw who it was.

She stepped back before he could see her. She silently prayed to the King for guidance. *What am I to do?* She walked closer to him, but Brogan grabbed her dress and started pulling her back.

"No, Brogan—let go! I cannot believe I'm saying this and I know we should just walk away, but I just can't."

She bent down and gently shook her feared enemy. "Wake up, Kavian!" He slowly opened his eyes and closed them again. He tried to move but he was too weak. Zoe examined him and discovered a big gash on his stomach and a large wound on his shoulder. *If I help him, he will only come after us,* she thought.

She stood up, turned around to leave, but Feena's words rang in her ears—"Maybe if someone would treat him kindly, perhaps he would change." She glanced once more at Kavian. His eyes were open now and he just stared at her helplessly.

I wonder where his so-called friends are? He closed his eyes and even looked peaceful.

I may regret this! Zoe used some of the King's water to clean his wounds, and then took some of the precious healing balm that Kieran had given her and applied it to his wounds. She bandaged them as best she could, and then opened his mouth to pour a little bit of water into it.

He began to stir and Zoe jumped back immediately. "Brogan, come on. I don't want him to see us." They started to walk away and then they heard a mumble.

"Don't go...please."

Zoe inched back to him cautiously, "What did you say?"

"Please, stay." He strained to speak, choking the raspy words out. "Why...why did you help me—after what I did to you?"

"I don't really know, except that we just could not leave you here to die."

"I don't understand—I...I would have left you to die. I did before."

Zoe kneeled down beside him and asked skeptically, "What happened to you?"

"I was in a fight with Antrum, Bantry, and some others." He coughed and then continued. "I picked up your scent beyond the

Cliffs of Fenner and tracked you." He stopped to catch his breath. "But I was repeatedly stopped by your friends and chased off your trail. I was on my way to get rid of you for good." He coughed again.

"The last time though, they caught me unaware and we fought." He breathed deeply as if willing himself to speak. "Bantry clawed me in the stomach and threw me up against a tree. I'm sure they thought I was dead....or would soon die."

He was beginning to feel better from the balm. "But I got up and followed your scent. I would have found you, but some strange animal shot me with an arrow in the shoulder and left me to die. I managed to pull it out and walked several miles until I could walk no further. I've been lying here ever since. By the way, what was in that water you gave me to drink? And my wound—the pain is leaving."

Zoe spoke up. "The water is from the King's well, and the healing balm was given to me by one of the King's servants."

Zoe heard a noise behind her and suddenly Antrum and Bantry ran up. Bantry clawed the ground. "Zoe, what are you doing? Why are you here with Kavian?"

Antrum was stomping his hoof on the ground. Before she could answer, he yelled, "And what about you Kavian, why are you here?"

Zoe confidently turned to Antrum and Bantry with resolve and said, "He was injured—I just couldn't leave him to die."

Bantry sharpened his claws and angrily said, "I know that Zoe—we were in a fight trying to help you! And what do you do? You stop to help the one who has been trying to kill you for months!"

"He seemed so pitiful and helpless lying there—it just seemed like the right thing to do."

"Zoe, we don't want you to get hurt. We're trying to protect you from Kavian."

"I know, I know," she shrugged.

Kavian eyed all of them and then willed his eyes closed as if he could change this predicament he was in. He was at their mercy for he was still too weak to even try to escape. But as he listened to them, something stirred inside that he had never felt before. What was it? His alleged friends hated him, and only obeyed him because he was stronger and they knew he could kill them. But Zoe and her friends seemed so different.

"Come over here, Bantry and Antrum, I want to talk to you alone." Zoe walked over to a nearby tree. "When I stayed with Feena, she once told me that she thought maybe Kavian would change if he was shown a little kindness."

Bantry was pacing and then stopped. "Zoe, but look at his past. What makes you think he would change now?"

"I don't really know—think about all our pasts. I have certainly changed since I first began my journey—maybe he can. I just think if by some miracle he wants to change, we should at least give him a chance to."

Bantry was watching every move Kavian made. "Look, there is more pressing business than this right now. We have another reason for coming to you."

"What is it Bantry?"

"There is a new leader of the triblens—his name is Jarleth. He is gathering every despicable creature he can find that follows Durgalt and they are heading this way for a war. They are using the excuse of getting revenge for what happened to Futney and Crendor as justification to kill you and any other follower of the King who gets in their way. This war has been building for many years."

"What are we to do? There is only you, Antrum, me, and Brogan to fight."

"No, this is not the case. Prince Arden is aware of Jarleth's plans. There are many who are coming to fight in the name of the King, including Feena, the elves—even the malios and fregors, and whoever else will join our cause."

"Malios and fregors?"

"Yes, they live in the land of Ferlan, not far from here. We thought maybe you would be there by now, but you must have been caught in the snowstorm and delayed, as we were. But tomorrow at this time, we should all be together. Evan has been keeping us informed of Jarleth's location. Fortunately, he is still a day behind us due to some fighting within his own army! But there is no time to delay. Arden should be arriving today in Ferlan by way of the Cashel River and we must be there before nightfall. Feena and many others went part of the way by the Cashel River and then a different route so they could gather together as many of the King's followers as possible."

They all thought Kavian was asleep, but he heard every word they said. He knew of this war, but he had hoped to kill Zoe first and get that out of the way. Is this what he wanted now? He listened as they continued to talk.

Bantry looked over at Kavian. "What are we to do about him? We cannot let him follow us."

Zoe whispered something that Kavian could not quite hear. His mind was raging inside. He could not believe that Zoe, of all people, would want to give him a chance. Did he really want to change? He had never really been happy working for Durgalt. He felt like he was always missing something. He looked at Bantry, Antrum, Zoe, and Brogan. They were friends—something he had never had. What would it be like to have a true friend? His vision seemed to clear and suddenly he knew that maybe this is what he always wanted. It would mean he would have to change from his evil ways. Is that even possible? He had been this way a long, long time.

Antrum had been listening to Bantry and Zoe, and he had an idea. "Well, I see both sides. Bantry has a very good point, Zoe. Kavian has been our enemy for as long as I can remember, so the only thing we do know about him is his past behavior. I also realize you want to give him a chance to change—that is assuming he even wants to. Before we jump to any conclusions here, we need to ask him. If he wants to change, I have a suggestion. We all abide in the forest by a code of honor. All the followers of the King abide by it. Once we speak our code of honor on a matter, it is sealed.

We cannot go back on it. I am sure Kavian is aware of this code as well. Do you really think he can change Zoe, follow this code, and the King?"

"For some strange reason I do."

"Bantry, what do you think?"

He pawed at the ground. "This is a tough call. I just don't like him! I know it's wrong but he has done some pretty mean things to my family—like trying to kill our cub!"

"Well, I know how that feels first hand. He has been trying to kill me for a while now," Zoe interjected. "Look at him—now is our chance to bring him to our side. Just think about what a great asset he would be in our war."

Bantry looked over at Kavian. "I can only say this. I'll be watching him constantly until I see a complete change in him. I'm taking no chances with anyone's safety."

"I agree—that would be wise," Antrum added. "All right then, we shall go talk with him."

Antrum cleared his throat and held his head high. "Kavian?"

"Yes," he answered weakly.

"Zoe seems to think you want to change. Is this true?"

Kavian held his head up as best he could. "I've been listening to all of you—hardly believing what I'm hearing." He labored to breathe but continued, "After Zoe helped me, I finally realized what I want—friends—real friends." Coughing, he added, "I know you don't trust me, and really, I can't blame you. I'm growing tired of following Durgalt. I realized that perhaps I can change my ways, but I'll need help. About the code of honor—I give my word of honor that I will not harm any of you in any way."

Zoe stood with her mouth gaping wide open as she listened in amazement. "Kavian, do you truly mean what you are saying?"

"Yes," he said with a longing, almost desperate look in his eyes.

Bantry spoke next. "We'll stay here for about an hour. That is all the time we can give you to regain some strength. We must go to Ferlan, and you can count that I'll be watching your every move. If you prove that you have truly changed, then you may stay with us."

Kavian looked at all of them gratefully, "You will see, I will change. I will serve you in any way I can."

Zoe was so astounded that she hardly knew what to say. She smiled and knelt down beside Kavian, touching his paw. "First get some rest—we will wake you shortly."

Kavian was so tired that he closed his eyes peacefully and was soon asleep. They all just stared at him and then at each other realizing that a miracle had just taken place. Grace, Antrum's mate, had stood in the background and heard everything. She walked up to Zoe and said, "This is a significant day. Because of your kindness Zoe, Kavian's heart changed toward us and the King—I believe Kavian is sincere. To have him on the King's side will prove a significant help in our battle against the enemy. It is a rare quality indeed to forgive when someone has treated you so wrongly, Zoe."

Everyone agreed. Zoe had forgiven, even when no one else was willing. This was a special day—one that would stay in their memories for a long time.

Zoe was still amazed at the change in Kavian. Unbelievably, he has turned to the good side! *The King will be happy about this— but I'm sure He already knows!* She just knew the King must have a very special plan for Kavian. The longing to be accepted had touched her heart. Zoe determined then to be what Kavian had never had—a friend.

Rejoicing, she decided to take a little walk and find a comfortable place to write in her journal about this memorable day, while Kavian was resting. After she had written for a while she looked up and saw something glimmering by an oak tree. She picked it up and saw that it was another gold key—the fifth! She read the inscription: **KINDNESS.** She placed it in her pocket for safekeeping. As she did this, she felt kindness increase in her heart—now she knew that it would continue to grow. Every trial she had been through had been worth it—for now her enemy Kavian had turned from his evil ways. His strength would be used in the war ahead, to their benefit—all due to a girl showing kindness to her enemy.

The key to kindness is bestowing gentleness combined with compassion.

Chapter Nineteen

For the grace of God has appeared,
bringing salvation to all men.
Titus 2:11

"Arden, you are not going to believe this, so sit down." They had just landed and tied their sailboat to a tree on the shores of Ferlan. Arden sat down on a nearby rock.

"What is it Evan?"

"Kavian has turned to the King's side! You will be amazed to learn who led him to the King."

Arden stood up with excitement. "It was Zoe, wasn't it?"

Evan laughed deeply. "Yes, my friend—none other than Zoe! If she can forgive Kavian for what he has done to her, then she has indeed matured greatly in the ways of the King. The power of her forgiveness changed Kavian, which is truly an amazing thing."

"I'm so proud of her! I can't wait to see her, Evan."

"Well, she should be here in a few hours."

"I wish I could go to her now, but our council meeting will begin soon."

Arden watched as the ships safely landed. There were many who had come to fight in this battle, but Arden still felt like the war would be difficult.

King Ronan walked over to his son. "Arden, do you have word about Zoe yet?"

"Yes, she is not far from here, Father."

"I must admit I am anxious to meet the one who has captured your heart. Do you still believe she's the one to be your bride?"

"I do, Father. If anything, this separation has confirmed even more the love I have for her."

King Ronan studied Arden. "She will be here soon enough. For now, we must think about the war ahead."

❈

Within an hour, Zoe and her friends were on their way. headed toward Ferlan, where she was to meet Arden and the others. She was so thankful she would not have to deviate from her map to their rendezvous point. Kavian had improved quickly due to the King's healing balm and water, and he was almost back to normal by the time they were ready to leave.

Suddenly, Kavian, Brogan, and Dapple's ears perked up as they heard the sound of many horses approaching. Zoe turned around and saw a group of seven men coming straight toward them. Before she could say anything, Bantry, Antrum, and Grace ran to see exactly who was coming. Zoe watched them bow. As the men advanced, they could clearly see they were dressed in the clothes of royalty. She focused on their leader, and when their eyes met, she knew immediately who He was.

Zoe nearly fainted. "It's Him! It is the King!"

Kavian wanted to run somewhere but it was too late—He was already in front of them.

As He approached, they could do nothing but bow. He stepped down from His horse and looked at all of them. When they saw Him face to face, they were astounded with His glory and majesty. He stood tall and assured. His face was clear, smooth, and pure. Compassion, kindness, and love flowed from His countenance toward them. He had friendly yet penetrating brown eyes, a slender nose, and strong chin. His brown hair fell at His shoulders and He wore a tan linen tunic, brown pants, and dark leather boots. As if to reassure them, He smiled. "Welcome My friends. Would you like to take a walk?"

None of them seemed able to speak because of the shock of seeing Him, so Zoe nodded her affirmation.

"Gabe, please hand Me the basket. Also, I would like for you to stay with the horses as I must visit with My friends for a few hours."

"Yes, my King."

"Follow Me. I want to take you to a favorite place of Mine."

Kavian stayed back at a distance from them as they walked.

The King turned to him and Kavian immediately put his head down. But when the King called his name, he looked up. "Kavian, come join us." He slowly walked up to them.

It was a short walk to a beautiful lake. Immediately, Zoe felt peace and rest flow into her. "This lake is called Placid Lake. Let your eyes take in the beauty and tranquility. Sit down my friends for I have prepared a special feast for you."

The King opened the basket, pulled out a blanket, and laid it on the ground. Then He put out more food than they had seen in a very long time. "This is a celebration meal. I have come to personally tell you Zoe that I am pleased with the progress of your journey. You have overcome many obstacles. Eat heartily My friends, and refresh yourselves with My water."

The King served each of them and then fixed His plate. As they were eating, the King continued to talk. He turned to Kavian with loving eyes, "First of all, let Me welcome you. I am pleased you have made the choice to turn from the evil one. You will be blessed for this. Are you ready to follow Me?"

When Kavian looked directly in the King's eyes, he could not help but feel His compassion. "Yes, I am."

"During the time ahead, Kavian, I will be with you, but you will not be able to see Me. You will have to trust that I am with you."

Kavian could hardly speak. "I never thought I would see You, and I will trust You. Thank You for letting me be Your follower— even after all the bad things I've done. I am very sorry. Please, if You will give me a chance, I will fight for You in this war. Just tell me what to do, and You can be sure I will do it. I no longer want the kind of life I had before."

The King smiled reassuringly at him. "Fine words Kavian, for I know they are from your heart. You have a purpose in your life which is about to unfold. Trust Me and you will see all that you are to do."

Kavian nodded and determined that he would.

The King then turned to Brogan. "You have been faithful in every way in serving Zoe. I have a gift for you." The King tapped the ground and said, "Come." Brogan obediently came and sat down.

He looked deeply into Brogan's eyes and then touched his throat and said, "Speak."

Brogan opened his mouth and he said his first word. "Z...Zoe."

Zoe ran and hugged him. "You said my name. You really said my name!" Her face shone with joy.

"My King, this is a gift for Brogan, but it's one for me too. Now I can talk to my devoted friend. Thank you so very much!"

The King smiled kindly at Zoe and then gazed warmly upon Brogan. "So, do you like being able to speak now?"

"I...I cannot believe it. I can talk! Thank you so much!"

"You are welcome. I know you will use this gift wisely."

"To be able to speak to Zoe in her language is a great gift— thank you, and I can now say that I want to follow You too."

"I knew this all along, but it is good to hear you say it. You are a great help to Me, and you will continue to serve the purposes of My kingdom."

He turned to Zoe next. "My Zoe! You have come so far in your walk, but there is still much more you need to learn before you reach My kingdom. I am pleased with your progress. What do you think is the most important lesson you have learned so far?"

Zoe thought for a moment. "I have faced fears that I never wanted to face, but I am getting over so many of them now, and I am learning to trust You in a deeper way. But I believe the most important lesson I have learned is to listen to my heart, because that is where You speak to me."

"You are right. If you will seek Me, you will find Me. Always listen carefully." His gaze penetrated deeply into Zoe eyes as He said the next words. "A war is almost upon My people Zoe. You will fight in this war and it will be difficult for you, but the greatest test of your walk will come after the war."

Zoe's heart became heavy. "What is this test?"

He answered with a question, "Will you trust Me in whatever comes?"

Zoe searched His eyes for an answer. "Yes, I will—in whatever comes."

"Good. In your walk, I have allowed you to make choices—good or bad. I will never force Myself upon you, but if you will remember to listen to My voice, I will show you the best choices for your life." He continued, "I will always help when you call upon Me."

Zoe tried not to sound worried. "I was hoping You could tell me a little something about this test."

"Do not worry. Remember that you can have peace in any situation as you so recently learned. The purpose of this test is for you to acquire the most important key of all."

Zoe laid aside the worry of the test. "My King, may I ask two questions?"

"Of course, My daughter."

"Will we win this war?

"Many of My followers who have asked for the gift of wisdom are in this war. They are even now holding a council meeting to discuss the strategy, and it is a wise one. If they hold to this strategy the war will be won. If they turn from it, then it will be lost."

"Then I will pray that they hold to the right strategy."

"What was your other question, Zoe?"

Somehow this question did not seem as important to Zoe with a war so close, but she decided to ask anyway. "I recently met Arden, Prince of the Elves in Runden Forest."

"Ah yes, My faithful friend."

"He has asked me to be his Princess. Is this what You desire for my life?"

"What does your heart say Zoe?"

Zoe searched her heart. "I care deeply for him, but I'm not sure. He said his father had a prophecy about his Princess to be, and he is certain it is me. Why am I not as convinced as he is?"

"Zoe, the time will come when you will know whether or not you should be his Princess. I will say this. You still have much to learn on your journey before it is the best time for you to marry.

Can you wait and see what the future holds while trusting Me to show you the best choice for your life?"

"Yes I can. I will do my best."

After they had enjoyed a meal of grand proportions including a special cake, they settled comfortably on the grass and listened to the King. Zoe prayed that her mind would be like good soil, ready for new seeds to be planted, ready for them to grow.

He talked to them more about following Him. "I am the Living Water. I am purifying you daily as you walk steadily forward. There will always be more to learn, so submit to whatever circumstances you are in, and learn all that you can from them. Also, always remember that you can overcome anything when you are following Me. Nothing can overcome you—unless you allow it to."

"Bantry, Antrum, and Grace, I am very pleased that you are learning to listen to My voice more clearly. Recently, the three of you prayed together and asked for more wisdom. I am giving you this gift today, which you will be able to use in the war ahead."

They bowed and thanked the King for the gift. Bantry spoke first. "Is there anything You can tell us that will help us in the war ahead?"

"Yes, now that you have asked. The triblens are bringing many gruelas which they plan to send first in the attack. Do not be afraid of them. They attempt to sow demonic whisperings of fear into others. Speak My name and they will flee from you. It is most important that you do this immediately for once you allow fear to control you, the war will be lost."

Antrum humbly came forward. "Thank you. We will share this wisdom with the others."

The King looked at Grace. "You have been faithful in praying for My people and I have drawn very close to you during this time. I am going to bless you and Antrum with two babies next year."

"Oh thank you my King. You know this has been my heart's desire for so long—to have children of my own." A tear fell from Grace's beautiful face as Antrum nuzzled her neck.

"Indeed dear King—this is quite a blessing for us. Thank you."

"You are quite welcome My friends."

"Bantry, your added gift of wisdom will enable you to step into a new leadership role this season. Use this wisdom to guide you."

Bantry bowed. "Thank you my King for this gift."

Then He turned to Zoe. "There have been many times in your journey that you became quite discouraged. In the future, turn to Me quickly for I am with you, and I will help you. But you must call on Me first." He took something out of His bag. "I have a special gift for you—the Book of My Words."

He handed the Book to her and she fingered it gently. It was not large but she felt deep inside that these were the most important words ever written. With heartfelt gratitude, she said, "Thank you. This means so much to me and I will treasure this Book always."

"By reading it at the beginning of the day, you will receive clarity of thought and nourishment for your soul. It will help you throughout the day. Read it at the end of the day and let My Words permeate deep within while you sleep. The more you read, the more you will become strengthened."

Zoe lovingly held the Book as though it was the most valuable treasure ever. And indeed it was. "I will be diligent to read this Book as much as I can. I have always wanted my very own—thank you so much." Zoe hugged Him and He laughed. She looked at the Book more closely. It had a light brown leather cover and the letters of her name were etched in gold on the cover—*Zoe Newbridge*.

"The next key I am giving you freely—the **Key to GOODNESS**. This key has many virtuous meanings. To have goodness within is to be pure, gentle, honest, kind, generous, and loving.

"Zoe, you displayed goodness when you helped Kavian, your enemy. You went beyond what you were feeling, dug deep into your heart, and forgave him. Then kindness developed in your character and you were able to extend this to Kavian. As you did, it grew even stronger deep wihtin you. Using these traits in your life will allow goodness to produce excellence within. It takes a lengthy time to mature, so I am giving the key to you now, so that it may take root in your heart."

The King handed her the key, and she touched the word, **GOODNESS.** She put the key in the pocket of her dress, and immediately, goodness melted into her heart as she felt the seed begin to grow.

"Thank you so much, but why was this key so easy to receive?"

"All of your keys have come at a cost. This key is freely given because it is what **I AM. I AM** Goodness. I give this key to all My friends who follow Me in a deeper way. Goodness is but a tiny seed in you now, but given My living water and food, it will grow strong and stand firm in your character. Do you understand now?"

"I think I do—the more I become like You, the more goodness will grow in me."

The King was pleased. "By this evening, you will be in the land called 'Ferlan' where many of My friends are awaiting you. The war is at hand, but do not fear for I am with you all. The time has come for Me to talk to some of My other followers about this impending war. But remember, I am with you always!"

They walked with Him to His horse and waved goodbye as He galloped off with His servants. Everyone stared at Him as long as He was visible.

Kavian grinned. "I cannot imagine being happier than I am right now. There is nothing I desire more than to serve the King."

Brogan was filled with excitement. "And listen to me—I can talk now! I can say anything I want!"

Brogan and Kavian pounced on each other playfully. "You two are something else!" *Yes, it was a wonderful day,* thought Zoe, *full of many incredible memories. I will never forget this day as long as I live!*

The key to goodness is to become more like the King, who is Goodness.

Part V
The
Great War

Chapter Twenty

*For our struggle is not against flesh and blood, but against the
rulers, against the powers, against the world forces of this darkness,
against the spiritual forces of wickedness in the heavenly places.*

*Therefore, take up the full armor of God, that you may be able
to resist in the evil day, and having done everything, to stand firm.*
Ephesians 6:12-13

Ferlan was beautiful. The sweet-smelling fragrance of
honey suckle filled the air. Gigantic trees loomed above,
spreading a canopy of shade from their massive leaves. It
was hard to believe that this wondrous place would be filled with
war all too soon. Zoe jumped off Dapple while Brogan looked at
her intently. "Are you afraid?"

"Brogan, if you had asked me that question a few months ago,
and I was getting ready to go fight in a war, I would have said yes,
but now I can honestly say that I'm not afraid. How can we be
afraid? We have just been with the King! Even if we died today, I
know where I will be for eternity, living with Him. But tell me, are
you afraid?"

"No, and I want you to know that I will protect you with my
life, Zoe. You are the best friend I have ever had. I hope we can
come out of this alive because there is so much I want to talk to
you about."

Kavian was listening to their conversation and was amazed at
the devotion Brogan had for Zoe. He wondered if he would ever
have a friend like that.

Prince Arden had just finished a long meeting with the council
when he saw Zoe. Immediately their eyes met, and neither moved.

King Ronan broke the moment with a laugh. "Son, do you want to greet her?"

Arden glanced at his father and grinned, then ran to Zoe and hugged her. Zoe enjoyed the security of being in the company of someone who cared so much for her. He whispered in her ear, "At last you're here. I've missed you more than you know."

King Ronan brought them out of their own little world when he spoke. "You must be Zoe. I'm King Ronan, Arden's father."

Zoe took her eyes off Prince Arden, only to see a double of him, yet older. She curtsied and replied, "I'm so pleased to meet you. Arden has spoken very highly of you."

"And I am pleased to meet you, my dear. Other than planning our strategy for this war, he has talked only of you. I'm glad you are here."

Arden realized that he needed to introduce the others to Zoe. "These are my friends, King Bevin of Vargo Valley, Keely of Parthalonia, and Mohan."

Zoe curtsied. "I'm honored to meet you all." She turned to Keely. "Parthalonia—that is just south of Brenlough, is it not?"

"Yes, it is."

"Well then, we are practically neighbors since my home is in Brenlough, so we must visit when I return."

Keely seemed surprised at her hospitality. "That would be most kind of you."

Arden was so proud of her for that comment. She had seen beyond the unusual appearance of Keely and saw him no differently than the others. *What an extraordinary maiden!*

Kavian realized at once that it was Keely, the strange animal who had shot him with an arrow after his recent fight with Antrum and Bantry recently. There were too many here that had been his enemies. Would they understand that he was not serving Durgalt anymore? Kavian was not sure, so he decided to hide in the bushes.

Zoe continued. "King Bevin, I have heard that Vargo Valley is a very beautiful place. I would love to visit there sometime."

"Please come anytime. Our land is known for its exquisite waterfalls."

"Then I will surely come!"

As Zoe greeted Mahon, she thought that next to the King, he had the most penetrating eyes she had ever seen.

Zoe extended her hands to her friends. "I would also like to introduce you to my friends. "This is Bantry, Antrum, his mate, Grace, Brogan, and my new friend, Kavian." Zoe turned to find Kavian but he was gone. "He was just here."

Arden looked puzzled. "I'll have a look around." Just as he was turning to go find him, Feena finally arrived. Zoe all but knocked Feena down when she saw her. "Feena, it is you! Oh, it's so good to see you!"

Feena grabbed Zoe and hugged her tightly. "T'is wonderful to see you too, lass! You have changed. Let me look at you more closely. T'is new strength that lights a fire in those beautiful eyes of yours. We have much to talk about."

Zoe smiled warmly. "Thank you, Feena. And I have learned so much, just like you said I would."

"Of this I was sure—now tell me, what have you learned?"

But before they could talk, everyone turned and watched many animals run into the glen—the fregors! As Zoe observed them, she was fascinated. Their faces were similar to that of a horse, but their muscular backs and legs looked like a lion. A dark brown fregor came forward. "My name is Kesh, leader of the fregors. I have brought sixty of our finest warriors to fight in the name of the King."

Prince Arden greeted him. "Come Kesh—bring all of your friends and meet everyone here." Introductions were made—except for Kavian. Arden was just getting ready to search for him again when another large group of animals arrived.

Zoe thought they were the most unusual animals she had ever seen. King Ronan whispered that they were the malios. They stood about three feet tall and walked on two feet. They had round tummies and were all different shades of soft-looking fur. They also had penetrating, large green eyes and rounded ears. Their whiskers seemed too large for their faces, and their noses twitched like rabbits. "Greetings in the name of our King. I am Cormac, leader of the malios and I have brought forty of my finest warriors."

Mahon shook Cormac's hand. "Thank you for bringing your warriors—all will be needed. I have heard about many battles that you have had with Kavian. Now my friend, we have a surprise for you. Kavian, come out."

Kavian knew he could hide no longer so he slowly came from behind the bushes slinking down as he walked. Not only had he just recently been in a battle with Cormac and Keely, he had also fought against many of the fregors and malios and had killed several of them. He felt quite ashamed now. Cormac lifted his sword.

"You have the audacity to show your face here!"

Mahon stepped forward to shield Kavian. "He will not fight you Cormac for he is now on our side."

Cormac seemed at a loss for words. "What?" Cormac just stared at Kavian. "How can this be? We fought no less than a week ago!"

Mahon touched the top of Kavian's head. "Cormac, believe me —Kavian has turned to our side and is no longer serving Durgalt."

From the intensity of Mahon's gaze, Cormac laid to rest his doubts and believed him. "Well then, I suppose that does make a difference." Cormac returned his sword in its sheath. "Forgive me, Kavian—I did not know."

"No, it is I who must ask your forgiveness, as well as everyone here. I cannot take back all of the awful things I've done, but I vow to you that I will do everything I can to right as many of those wrongs as I can, by fighting with you for the King's honor."

Keely as well as everyone else who had dealings with him from the past came forward and received his apology. Kavian's humbleness in admitting he had been wrong and asking their forgiveness did much to heal the many wounds that they had suffered from him.

King Ronan called for everyone's attention. "Come, you must be tired and hungry. Please refresh yourselves with the food that is already laid out for you. When everyone has finished eating, we have much to do. This may be the last meal we have for a while, so eat heartily for the war draws nigh. You must also take time to fill your flasks with water from the river so you will not thirst in the hours of fighting to come."

Zoe walked to King Ronan and quietly spoke something in his ear. He listened intently and then signaled for everyone to listen.

"My friends, I must speak to you again. Zoe has just informed me that she has a bottle of the King's living water. As many of you know, this water never runs dry and has healing and rejuvenating properties that will give us strength to fight. I am pleased to say that she will share it with us. Bring your flasks to her and she will fill them with His refreshing water."

There were around five hundred flasks to fill, but with Arden's help, Zoe was able to quickly accomplish the task. After everyone ate, it was time to reveal the council's strategy.

Mahon stood. "My friends, many of you may be wondering why the King is not here to fight this battle for us. But the fact is, He is here! His Spirit lives within all of us, which means we have the power of His gifts within us. The way we use these miraculous powers is by faith, and for the good of His kingdom. Durgalt has drawn powers from the depths of evil and has bestowed them upon witches, warlocks, gruelas, triblens, and other evil creatures that will use them for corruption. Realize that we are fighting against spirits of darkness, which rule our enemies, not their flesh and blood. These dark powers within them in no way compare to the power of light that the King has given us. Keep that in mind as you fight.

"Evan has just returned and informed me of some very important information. Jarleth and his creatures are planning to attack us at midnight. It nearly cost him his life to find out this news. A witch cast a spell that took the breath out of him, causing him to lose the power to fly. But fortunately, he quickly prayed to the King and was set free from the spell. This is just one example of the evil powers that Durgalt has given his followers to use. The powers the King has given us are far greater—but you must remember to use them! There are approximately five hundred of us to fight for our King. Evan counted more than six hundred of our enemies, but there is nothing to fear—the King is on our side!

"Some of you may not be aware of the gruelas that breed in Hemlock Forest. Evan told me that Jarleth plans to send them out first in the battle. Zoe, you have dealt with these wicked creatures. Please, give our friends any guidance that will help to conquer them."

Zoe stepped forward. "The gruelas are nothing but shadows of darkness that attempt to sow their own fears into their victims. The King advised us not to listen to their demonic whisperings or we will be useless in this war. If we let fear control us, the war will be lost. I know this firsthand. When you see them, call upon the King's name, and they will flee because they cannot stand to be in the presence of Courage Himself."

Mahon continued. "Indeed this is helpful. The time for war is almost here. You must listen carefully and pay heed to this strategy. I too have some vital information to share. Each of you have spiritual gifts—use them this day! Now, as I call your gifting, separate into that group.

"Archers, come forth! Half of you will go first in battle and half of you will stay in the rear. As you lead the way, shout forth the praises of our King and destroy the enemy at a distance, shooting down fear with your bow and arrows. When the demonic gruelas come, use your shields of faith for protection and call upon the King's name and they will leave. Apply your faith at the beginning to guide you, and then throughout the battle. Maintain your faith and use it at the end when many may become weak and begin to doubt. You must not grow weary or back down, but continue to destroy our enemies by not missing your mark. With faith, you must believe that everything is possible. Therefore, we have already won the battle. Keep this alive in your hearts throughout this war!

"Swordsmen, come forth! A third will be in the front, a third in the middle, and a third in the rear. The King has given you the strategies of wisdom, knowledge, and understanding to wage war. Use your swords to thrust them into the enemy while guiding those around you with your decisive courses of action. Do not lose ground! Speak light into dark places and strike our enemies so they will fall. Keep the faith and believe that we have won the victory!

"Spearmen, come forth! You will be dispersed throughout. Call upon the King all through the battle to reveal strategies and words of life for our warriors. Petition the King to give strength to the weary from the beginning of the battle until the end. You must give words of encouragement to those around you while you spear the enemy with truth and cut him to the quick. Then watch the enemy fall on every side!

"Shield warriors, come forth! You will also be dispersed in every place. Faith is your shield and it works with love. It is our greatest defense against evil. Love conquers everything, so you must shield those around you. For the love of the King, we are fighting to bring peace to our land, upholding truth, while conquering our enemies. Remember that LOVE NEVER FAILS!"

Mahon looked around at the menagerie of troops. All the King's followers were mixed together according to their giftings—elves, malios, fregors, the Parthalonians, humans, and various animals, and they all manifested resolute steadfastness in their eyes. "We must lay any burdens down and accept the King's peace. Our last and most important strategy now is to pray in unity." Everyone bowed their heads.

"Our King, we ask for Your guidance in this war. Though we are outnumbered, we believe in faith that the victory is ours. You have called us together, and we are here to fight in Your name. Help us stand firm in Your truth. Cover and protect us so that none of the spells of the witches and warlocks are able to affect us. In faith help us with courage to destroy our enemies. Send us Your peace and wisdom to guide us in this war. Watch over these warriors, My King, and let Your will be done."

Mahon opened the King's Book. "There are many crucial Words in this Book. Hide these Words in your heart so they might be recalled as you battle. Listen to these Words:

> *...He is their strength in time of trouble...He delivers*
> *them from the wicked, and saves them,*
> *because they take refuge in Him.*
> *Psalm 37:39-40*

> *Therefore, my beloved brethren, be steadfast, immovable,*
> *always abounding in the work of the Lord, knowing that*
> *your toil is not in vain in the Lord.*
> *I Corinthians 15:58*

> *"And they will fight against you, but they will not overcome you,*
> *for I am with you to deliver you," declares th e LORD.*
> *Jeremiah 1:19*

"Keep these words in your heart as you fight and remember the King is your strength—He will deliver you from all of your enemies because you take refuge in Him. Believe this! Be steadfast and do not let the enemy take any ground. In faith, we will win this war!"

Evan flew down and had a quick word with Mahon. "My friends, Evan has just informed me that it will be minutes before our enemies are here. Stand firm in your faith, and make ready your weapons, for the war draws nigh!"

Courage overcomes fear with steadfast faith.

Chapter Twenty-One

And the LORD is the one who goes ahead of you;
He will be with you. He will not fail you or forsake you.
Do not fear, or be dismayed.
Deuteronomy 31:8

The air was thick with concentration as the King's followers prepared for war. The archer's brows were furrowed with unwavering concentration as they drew back their bows, ready to release the arrows at the first sight of their enemies. Swords, daggers, and spears were drawn. Shields were in place as they continued to wait. Mahon walked back and forth encouraging the lines to stand firm and hold their ground. "The King is with us brave warriors—do not fear, but concentrate. With faith we shall see His victory!" The sound of their enemy's footsteps intensified as they drew closer.

Mahon climbed high on a cliff and continued to direct his friends. When he could see the enemies approach, he shouted, "The time has come! Archers—release your arrows!"

As the arrows met their targets, more than fifty of the enemy fell. The gruela's dark shadows quickly ascended with deep murmurings of fear and hopelessness ringing through the air. Their effect was chilling. But before it could overpower the soldiers of the King, Mahon told them to shout the King's name at the gruelas and crush their evil words.

Over and over they shouted words of faith and encouragement. "Our King is victorious! He is Ruler of all! He is above all! Our King is awesome!" The gruelas quickly left, but Mahon knew they would be back. As the archers continued to shoot, they knocked down nearly one hundred more of their enemies. The enemy shot back but only five of the King's army fell due to the protection of their shields.

The evil horde pressed on until the two armies were face to face and the clash of swords and spears began. Zoe was standing on the wide limbs of a large oak tree, and sent arrow after arrow into the enemy line with deadly accuracy. She saw the gruelas advancing again, and checked her shield as she quivered at the horrendous sight. She ignored them, and shot down ten more triblens. As she concentrated on her shooting she was not aware that she had been sighted by the one who most wanted her dead.

As Jarleth saw Zoe, he forgot all about the rest of the battle and he focused on the girl warrior. When she finally saw him he was nearly on top of her. His evil smirk and blood-shot eyes almost took her breath away. She grabbed a branch to keep from falling. "At last I will get revenge!" Jarleth shouted.

Arden, who was intentionally staying close to Zoe, heard Jarleth and spun around. Quickly, he slung his bow across his back and drew his sword, running as fast as he could to her defense. As Arden lifted his sword to drive it through Jarleth, a blow to his stomach sent Arden sprawling to the ground. In a flash the dark lord raised his sword to finish Arden. But more swiftly still, Zoe took quick aim and released her arrow, hitting Jarleth in his lower back. The sword fell from his hand as he dropped to the ground in agony. Arden rolled over and in a single swift motion, thrust his sword through Jarleth's stomach. As he pulled his sword out, Jarleth's life drained from him.

Arden silently thanked the King and looked up at Zoe, who was obviously doing the same. They locked eyes for a moment, but the loud and close screeching of the triblens drew their attention back to the conflict that was now raging all around them.

From his cliff, Mahon could see the gruelas were affecting some of the malios. He proclaimed with a thundering voice, "Use your shields, malios! Trust the King and you cannot lose. We have the victory—now use your spears! Fight in the name of the King!"

The malios raised their shields and their resolve rose with them as the smallest warriors on the field held their ground under a horrendous onslaught. Already a dozen malios lay dead or mortally wounded. Cormac, their captain, hurled his spear with all of the strength he could muster at one of the largest triblens. It hit its mark and the shriek of the giant triblen filled the air. A fregor ran to the stunned giant, stood on his two feet, knocked the triblen to the ground and began stomping the life out of him. The other malios and fregors then began to do the same, working together until the triblens began to give way before them.

Mahon moved from point to point along the lines, encouraging the weary, and directing them to stand their ground, waiting for the chance to exploit a weakness and sound the charge. He was not willing to just turn back the evil horde, he was determined to defeat the enemy completely and restore the peace of the land. As he was searching for such an opportunity, he saw a dozen witches and warlocks surrounding Ronan, Bevin, and Arden.

Mahon felt that something was wrong as he watched them over the knoll to his right. An eerie silence from that direction convinced him that he needed to move fast. He prayed to the King, ran to the cliff, and seeing the situation, jumped right into the center of the conflict. The witches and warlocks were so stunned at first that half of them retreated in terror. The others became enraged, spewing forth curses and incantations so foul and loud that it drew the attention of all of the combatants around them. It took all of Mahon's concentration to see through the darkness that began to engulf them, as he breathed, "In the name of the King, in the name of the King..."

Each side examined the other, waiting for someone to make a move. Two of the warlocks looked fairly normal on the outside, but Mahon knew better for evil was set deep in their eyes. Three of the four witches were quite beautiful, but as with the two warlocks, their eyes gave away the deep evil that was within them. The fourth witch was humped over, with scraggly, oily hair. The gruelas also began to inch their way closer, waiting to seize their victims.

Ronan, Bevin, and Arden began to weaken due to the spells. Each began to slowly lower his shield. As the gruelas pressed in closer, whispering words of defeat and fear, the three royal leaders weakened even further as they lowered their weapons too— confusion and fear were beginning to grip them hypnotically. The witches and warlocks lifted their swords, preparing to strike. Suddenly, Mahon began shouting at the witches and warlocks in a language that none of the vile ones had ever heard. When he did this all of their curses seemed to come back on them, now gripping them with confusion and fear. At the same time, Bevin, Ronan, and Arden stood up straight, with their minds beginning to clear, and quickly fell upon their enemies. With a precise thrust of their swords, the witches and warlocks quickly died from the throes of their own curses and spells.

Mahon gave a word of thanks to the King, and summoned Ronan, Bevin, Arden, the elves, and many of the Parthalonians to help the swordsmen and spearmen who were beginning to fall back. Mahon raced about telling everyone to stand, and to speak words of faith and encouragement to one another. The Parthalonians shot their arrows with deadly accuracy, causing the enemy to fall all around them. Soon the lines were holding, and in some places a slow advance began. With each step forward it seemed that increased strength came into them.

Mahon found that the shield warriors were not only holding their ground, but they had begun to use short daggers to bring down any of the enemy foolish enough to get close to them. Soon they had formed such an impregnable front that when any of the soldiers of the King began to falter they would gather behind the mighty shields and regroup before going back into the fracas, face to face.

Meanwhile, Zoe noticed Kavian and the wolves in some bushes behind the battlefront. When she heard a strange wolf speaking, she stopped to listen.

"What are you doing here, Kavian?"

"I follow the King now."

"You? Ha! You're lying! The King would never have you on His side. You are more foul than any of the witches and warlocks."

"That was true, but that is no longer who I am. He forgave me and He will forgive you too if you ask Him."

"You fool! No one can forgive like that. It's a trick. Now come back where you belong and fight with us. We can end this war for good. You'll be the hero and leader of the dark side, which you were always meant to be. We need you. They're just using you and in the end they'll surely torture you for all that you have done to them."

Kavian began to ponder what Tiff was saying. Certainly it seemed reasonable. Tiff continued to implore him, "Come on, we don't have much time. You can bring about the victory and you know our master will reward you handsomely. Tell him that you joined the other side as a ploy."

Kavian stood silent for a moment. "Tiff, even if everything you say is true, I would rather be tortured by the King than rewarded by Durgalt. The little time that I've been on the King's side is better than anything I've known before in my whole life. I have peace and I've tasted a joy I never even knew existed. I would rather be the King's fool than Durgalt's hero."

Tiff was so stunned that he did not know how to answer. Then his nostrils flared, he bared his teeth, and jumped Kavian, knocking him to the ground. Tiff was younger and stronger, but Kavian was more experienced, and it did not take him long to pin Tiff to the ground.

"Tiff, you have been a loyal friend, even though we were cohorts in darkness. I implore you, you can have what I have. You don't know what real love is, but trust me, it's like nothing we've known before."

As Kavian talked to his former young lieutenant, he did not notice that twenty other wolves had begun circling them, ready to pounce on Kavian. Bantry saw what was happening, let out a piercing roar, and quickly jumped two wolves at once, knocking them both to the ground with one pounce. Antrum was right behind him, stabbing as many as he could with his knife-like antlers. A huge mangy wolf jumped on Antrum's back, but Zoe was able to get a clear shot, killing the wolf instantly. Between Bantry and Antrum attacking, and Zoe sending arrow after arrow with perfect accuracy, soon dead wolves were strewn all about the ground. Brogan also had been fighting two other wolves and now had them running. He chased them briefly, and then rejoined the bloodshed around Kavian. Though he was young, his speed and raw courage were too much for the enemy wolves, and they began to retreat in disorder.

Mahon shouted to Antrum and Bantry, "You must help the malios and fregors. They are weakening and the triblens are about to break through." They left but shouted to Zoe that they would return as soon as they could. They were hardly out of sight when the wolves reappeared.

Zoe shot two wolves so quickly that at first the others did not know what had felled them. She tried to get a shot at Tiff, but he lunged at Kavian and soon they were so entangled she could not get a clear shot without the risk of hitting Kavian. Then Brogan jumped into the fray. Tiff easily knocked Brogan off, but he jumped back in trying to help Kavian. Zoe was helpless. She quickly prayed for the King's help before her attention was turned to a deafening bellow behind her. A huge black bear with razor sharp claws extended was about to jump Kesh, who had frozen in fear. Immediately, Zoe aimed and shot the bear in his hind leg and he retreated with a yelp. Next she shot a bear that was attacking Cormac and his partner. He, too, quickly retreated before the agonizing arrows.

Zoe looked back to Brogan, Kavian, and Tiff, but she still could not get a good shot. Tiff was fighting as if possessed by a legion. There was so much blood now that she was afraid if she did not get a shot at Tiff soon, both Kavian and Brogan would not last very much longer. She yelled for Arden but there was no response. Tormented by frustration when she saw another wolf sneaking up, she dispatched a shot quickly, killing him instantly.

The battle between Kavian, Brogan, and Tiff continued to rage for another hour. *Where does Tiff get this much strength to fight?* Her frustration was mounting because she could still not get a shot at Tiff. She could see that Kavian was weakening fast. Tiff would soon be at his throat and would finish him. Where was Brogan? Then she saw him—lying in a pool of blood. "Oh no!" she screamed above the clamor of the battle, giving away her position to all of the enemies in the wood.

Arden had told her to stay in the tree and not leave for any reason, but she just had to help Brogan. She made a decision. She jumped down from the tree, leaned forward, and aimed at Tiff. But before she could release her arrow, he jumped and knocked her down. He was going for her neck to put an end to her quickly, but Kavian flung himself on Tiff knocking him off of her. As Tiff turned to curse his old mentor, Kavian, Zoe sent off her shot. It hit the mark. Tiff looked over at her, and then Kavian, as he slumped to the ground.

The other wolves that had been sneaking up saw their leader fall. Zoe saw them and was about to start letting the arrows fly when they began to run. She did not see the bears, but Arden, who had come running when he heard Zoe's cry, saw them and yelled, "Zoe, get back in the tree!"

Zoe was crying. "No! I have to help Brogan and Kavian. Look at them!"

Arden shouted again, "Get in that tree—now!"

Zoe had never heard Arden speak with so much authority and she swiftly did as he said, which saved her from the lunge of a huge bear. She quickly aimed and shot two arrows that sent the bear staggering back into the woods. Arden saw that she was safe so he quickly ran back to help the spearmen and swordsman. She looked around, and could see no danger so she climbed down and ran to Brogan.

As she lifted his head into her lap, she saw Kavian leaning over Tiff, talking to him. "Even now Tiff, if you swear allegiance to the King, He will receive you."

Gasping for air, she heard Tiff's response, "How? How could He receive me? I have nothing to give Him now. What good would my allegiance be? I…I…have hated Him and tried to destroy His work my whole life. There is no w…way that He would ever receive me."

Kavian did not give up. "It has nothing to do with what we can do for Him, but just being humble enough to accept what He can do for us. I don't know much about Him yet, but I do know that this is all it takes. Please Tiff."

But it was too late—Tiff was gone. Kavian laid down beside him, praying that He had given allegiance to the King before he died, but he would never know. Kavian was too weak to get up, lying in his own blood. Zoe was amazed by what she heard. She carried Brogan over to Kavian and laid him down by his side. With her hand she gently brushed the fur on his head. "Kavian, you're a noble creature. You must not die. The King has much for you to do."

Kavian was too weak to even look up at her. He felt that his life was slipping away. He could see Brogan, who looked like he had already passed away. He then looked at Tiff and then the other wolves that he could see strewn about. *I've got to live*, he thought. *I've got to save the others*. With that his eyes closed.

Arden was trying to get back to Zoe when a warlock blocked his path. He was an old one who had wrinkles in his wrinkles. He was mumbling something Arden could not understand, but it caused a fog to envelop him like a blanket. His knees became weak and he started to sway. Arden then recalled the power of Mahon's words and quickly repeated what he could remember, shouting them. As he spoke the words, new strength came upon him and the fog lifted quickly, Arden saw the old warlock stagger, as if something was choking him. Terrible noises came from deep in his throat. Arden felt as if the demons that were in the warlock were now raging against the old man they had possessed. They were choking him to death and he began to grovel in the dust in terrible agony. Arden drew his sword and thrust it through him, more out of pity than wanting to kill him.

Shocked by the sight, Arden started for Zoe again. She was still leaning over Kavian and Brogan, with tears streaming down her cheeks. She could not believe that they were both dead. But through her tears she could see Feena in a fierce battle with a witch.

Evan flew over and called to Zoe. "Mahon has sent word that you must get back in the battle. We need your help. You are a warrior of the King. You cannot stop until the war is over."

It was then that Arden stepped up beside her and gently raised her up. He looked down at Kavian and Brogan, and then at the other dead and wounded. Then he looked into her eyes and said, "I'm sorry. They died well. We cannot let them die in vain. Evan is right. You are a mighty warrior and we need you in this fight. In the King's name, we will prevail for our friends!"

She felt she could hardly breathe because her grief was so great. She was just too weak to fight any more, but she took a deep breath, picked up her bow, and started back to her post. As she walked with determination to continue this fight, she felt strength come back into her. She looked through the haze and saw Feena was still in a terrible fight with the witch. She started toward them and felt resolve growing with each step. A single shot felled the witch. Feena, breathing heavily, turned to thank Zoe, but she was already walking away toward the sound of battle. Feena was amazed by the focus on Zoe's face, grabbed her bow, and then followed.

"Thanks, Zoe—t'was good timing for sure!" As Feena caught up to her, Zoe reached out and squeezed her hand without even slowing down. They came upon King Bevin who was cornered by two bears. Zoe shot one and Feena the other.

"That was a close one girls. Thanks!" As King Bevin looked at Zoe, he too was surprised by the look of resolve in her face. He jumped up and followed the two, sensing that something was about to happen. Arden was also following behind, watching it all.

As they crested a little knoll, Zoe stopped to look around. The dead were strewn all over the ground. The soldiers of the King were still fighting valiantly, but they were weary, and still facing a seemingly endless horde of the evil one's raging dark warriors.

Prince Arden caught up to Zoe, Feena, and King Bevin just as they entered the front lines of the battle. Zoe and Feena were releasing arrows with fatal accuracy as fast as they could pull them out of their quivers. The advancing enemy was stunned and came to a quick stop. The enemy had not supplied his troops with shields, so they were completely vulnerable, falling with great cries of pain, rage, and terror. The effect was chilling up and down the lines. Zoe saw the opportunity and raced forward to the attack. Then all the warriors along the entire line began to charge. The enemy's lines began to retreat—then they began to flee. Panic gripped the entire army of the enemy and there was no way for their leaders to stop their flight.

Within an hour the evil horde was so scattered that there were hardly two left together anywhere. Their abandoned weapons were scattered over miles of territory. They swam rivers, fled into the forest, and tried to hide in bushes or trees. Some would not stop running until far into the night. By morning there would be no more of the evil horde left anywhere within the boundaries of those who served the King.

Unwavering faith, courage, and perseverance
result in victory every time!

Chapter Twenty-Two

We will sing for joy over your victory,
And in the name of our God we will set up our banners...
Psalm 20:5

Mahon stood high above on the cliff late the next day surveying the remaining small clashes that were taking place in the valley below, far beyond Ferlan. It would soon be completely over.

Everyone had gathered to hear what Mahon had to say. "We have won this war in the name of the King!" he said. "We were confident of victory, but this is beyond our greatest expectations. The song of this triumph will be sung for many years throughout the land. Many of Durgalt's followers will surrender now to the King." The crowd cheered as Mahon congratulated them on their bravery and endurance.

It was getting dark so Prince Arden began looking for Zoe. After a time he happened upon Feena, who was also looking for Zoe.

"T'was soon after the breakthrough I last saw her, but occupied I was for the next few hours chasing the enemy. Where she went, I do not know. But worried I am not—that lass can take care of herself."

"Of that I am sure," the Prince answered, smiling as he thought of her remarkable attack on the enemy, sparking the victory right when it had looked the most desperate for the servants of the King. "Feena, you taught her well."

"Arden, my lad, what we saw in Zoe today cannot be taught. We saw the strength she has always had. It's when we are in our most difficult battles that our true strength will shine. Proud of her, I am. I wonder if she is still chasing the enemy?"

Prince Arden thought for a minute, and then said, "I feel confident she did, but after that she probably went back to check on her friends, who I'm afraid are dead."

Feena replied, "T'is right you are, I believe."

⟿ ✳ ⟾

While everyone was shouting the victory, Zoe ran to Brogan and Kavian. To Zoe's relief, Brogan moved his head slightly when he saw her, but the deep gash in his neck was so large that he could barely move. Zoe was so happy he was alive that tears fell from her cheeks all over Brogan. She quickly washed the deep wound in the King's living water and applied the healing balm to the wound. She also gave him the living water to drink. When he finally spoke she cried. "Thank you Zoe—I'll be fine now. Go help Kavian." Zoe quickly kissed his brow and bent over to check on her new friend.

To her amazement, she saw Kavian's chest rise and fall weakly. She gave thanks to the King and gently wiped his blood-matted head and neck, washing his wounds with the living water. She used all the healing balm on what wounds she could, but soon realized there would not be enough to cover all his injuries.

"Oh, Kavian, if only I could have shot Tiff sooner, he would not have done this to you! You fought so bravely against Tiff and the other wolves! And thank you my friend for saving my life." She kissed his brow. A verse in the King's Book came to mind as she bathed his wounds, and she spoke the words so Kavian could hear.

> *Greater love has no one than this, that one*
> *lay down his life for his friends.*
> *John 15:13*

Kavian had at last learned to love. Zoe would never forget the devotion she had seen in him. It was for the love of the King and his new friends that he fought so bravely.

Zoe kept talking to him but he did not respond. He only lay motionless, and she cried as she had never cried before. "Please, Kavian, please try to live! You have so much more to do!"

Zoe earnestly begged the King to hear her prayer. "Please dear King, spare his life for he has only just begun to know You. I entreat You, please let him live!"

Kavian opened his eyes. Fresh tears flowed down Zoe's cheeks. At least she would have a little more time with him. She gave him some of the King's water to drink, but it hurt too much for him to swallow and it dribbled out of his mouth onto the ground. With all the tenderness of a mother, she continued to bathe his wounds, cleaning out the dirt deep within.

He stirred a little and he whispered, "I—I shall never forget—your kindness, Zoe."

Zoe cried uncontrollably as she watched Kavian struggle to breathe. All she could find to say was, "I love you!"

Kavian weakly looked at Zoe, and then she saw his tears. She could not have known that no one had ever said those words to him before. All she could see was his suffering. She knew his blood loss was too much as she watched Kavian strain more and more to breathe, but there was nothing she could do to help him.

Arden and Feena had both been treating many of the wounded. Even though they wanted to go to Zoe, they just could not pass them by. Feena finally said, "To Zoe you must go Arden. I'll stay and attend to the wounded. Now go."

When he finally found her she was praying, stopping only to wipe the brow of the dying Kavian. When Arden saw how injured Kavian was, he immediately called his father to come pray for Kavian. Zoe smiled through tears, "Of course, Arden!" and hugged him gratefully.

King Ronan had been praying for the many who were wounded, but quickly came when Arden called him. Zoe spoke first. "Will you pray for Kavian?" she sobbed.

"Why certainly I'll pray for him and I'll call others to pray as well." About ten elves gathered around Kavian. Even Mahon came. King Ronan laid his hands on every wound while praying to the King. "We beseech You dear King to save our friend, Kavian. He has not known You long, but his desire is to serve You. Will You now come and heal this one who so willingly fought today? In Your name we pray." As they continued to pray, Kavian's eyes fluttered open.

He looked around, suddenly realizing that he was going to live! He was so overcome with emotion that he could hardly speak. "Thank you—thank you all! Now I know for certain that love is stronger than death."

Even though his strength was returning, he could say no more because of the deep emotions he was feeling. Never had he even dreamed that anyone would care for him in this way—and these were the very ones he had hated and tried to kill!

Zoe bent down and hugged him with tears of joy streaming down her face. "You fought so courageously for the King, and I am so proud to call you my friend." As Kavian gazed at Zoe and the others, he smiled realizing that at last he had found what he had never had before—true friends.

Brogan limped over to Kavian and grinned as only a wolf can. "I never knew my own father, but I would have been proud to have a father as courageous and wise as you."

Kavian was now sitting up. He scratched his paw on the ground. "Thanks Brogan. That means a lot to me. Your mother must have been a fine wolf to have raised such a fine son as you. Zoe said you were born in Hemlock Forest. You know I lived there too, but I never saw you. Who was your mother?"

"My mother's name was Reesa. I remember her well and you are right, she was a fine wolf."

At first Kavian looked confused. Then he seemed to be counting something. "You are one year old—is that right?"

"Yes, almost a year and a half now."

Then a look that bordered on shock crossed Kavian's face. He tried for a moment to speak but it was almost as if he had forgotten how. Everyone was watching him. Then as huge tears spilled down his face, he whimpered, "Brogan—you are my son!"

In His Light, truth will be revealed.

Chapter Twenty-Three

It was for freedom that Christ set us free;
therefore keep standing firm
and do not be subject again to a yoke of slavery.
Galatians 5:1

The victory celebration lasted well into the night. It would likely have lasted much longer had everyone not been so weary from the war. They had brought all of the wounded and gathered them around the campfires where praying and rejoicing was speeding their recovery. When the news about Kavian and Brogan spread to another campfire it brought the rejoicing to an even higher crescendo.

"I need to talk to you, Zoe." Arden grabbed her hand and gently pulled her to a fallen log where they could sit. "I have been doing a great deal of thinking. I realized today while we were fighting the enemy, I have not fully trusted the King to protect you—I was trying to take care of you in my own strength. I now know that part of loving you is releasing you to be who you are meant to be. I just could not let go of you. I wanted you with me so much that I didn't even want you to finish your journey to Remiah. I was selfish and I need to ask your forgiveness."

Zoe leaned over and kissed Arden on the cheek. "Thank you Arden. This means so much to me. You were protecting me because you love me, but even in the short time we have known each other I have felt a little smothered. I was concerned that if I was to be with you there would be no freedom for me to be who I am called to be—but only what you wanted me to be, your Princess. I am so close to finishing the journey now—you know I must complete it."

"I really do want you to finish your journey. Will you return to me after you go to Remiah?"

"Yes, if I believe it is the King's will for me."

He longed to understand her more. "You do not sound certain."

Zoe looked down and then at Arden again. "I care for you a great deal Arden, but I still do not know for certain that I am to be your wife. You are the most thoughtful man I have ever known. You are handsome, and you are already an exceptional leader of your people. You are a great warrior who I believe will always fight for what is right. You are everything a girl could ever dream of in a husband, but I do not feel ready to marry. I don't know what's missing, but something is. I hope to discover what it is so that I can return to you, and feel everything for you that I must."

"Then, I'll wait as long as it takes because there will never be anyone for me but you."

Zoe smiled. "I hope things will work out for us because I don't believe anyone will *ever* love me as much as you do. I am truly honored, Arden."

Arden took her in his arms and whispered, "I believe the day will come when you will love me just as I love you."

Zoe whispered back, "I pray that day will come, too."

Feena, Antrum, and Bantry were still helping those hurt in the battle when Zoe and Arden arrived to help. Zoe walked over to Feena and hoped to have a long visit with her, once they finished redressing the wounds of the injured. She was disappointed when Feena told them she had to leave due to an urgent message from Evan—a new pack of wolves were just spotted in Hemlock Forest.

"T'is wonderful to have seen you again, Zoe. When the enemy is cast out of one place, another place he will always attack, and with great rage. Guard I must what the King has given me to watch over. We will get together just as soon as we can. The best is yet to come—from Remiah you are not far now. "

Feena grabbed Zoe and hugged her tightly. "T'was proud of you I was in the battle, lass. You fought like a great warrior—t'is what you are now! Much you had to overcome to get where you are now." Feena lifted Zoe's chin. "Remember, the chosen path you must stay on and do not let anything stop you from reaching your destiny." Feena hugged her one last time and waved goodbye. Zoe watched quietly as she walked away in the distance.

It took until early in the morning to finish re-bandaging and caring for those who were hurt. Even though it was much work, the rejoicing was making the task easier because there was so much joy. While Arden, Zoe, and many others worked, Kavian and Brogan rested until evening. When Zoe and Arden found them, they were frolicking under the shade of a willow tree. Zoe laughed, "I would say the two of you are feeling pretty spunky now!"

Kavian's heart was so full he could hardly speak without getting choked up. "Zoe, thank you again—for everything. I am at your service now, and I will protect you with my life. It's not far to Remiah, and if you will have me, I would like to see that you arrive there safely."

"Along with me too, of course." Brogan added.

"I am truly thankful to have friends as devoted as you two. Kavian, I have been feeling that you are supposed to go with us on this journey. So yes, please come with us!"

Arden bowed. "I'm grateful to you both—I know she will be in good keeping."

While they were talking, King Ronan joined them. "Mahon would like to speak to all of us in the thicket now. Come, and afterwards we shall talk."

When everyone was seated, Mahon began. "My friends, we are living in memorable days for they will be marked in history as a great victory for the King. You bravely fought in faith, and for this you shall be rewarded in due time. There are some who died, but they did not die in vain. Because of their bravery and yours, freedom has come to this land. The enemy no longer rules Ferlan." Everyone gave a great shout.

Mahon scanned the crowd intently. "My friends, there was more to this war than I believe you realize. Ferlan is the last flatland before the mountains in Remiah. For years, the enemy has controlled Ferlan, making it most difficult for any of the King's followers to reach their final destination of Remiah. We have taken this land in the name of the King, and His followers shall pass here in peace. Now, we are here to help them on their way."

This brought another shout and cheer from the warriors. Mahon waited to speak until it was quiet. "I was not surprised at how swiftly this war was won. When we first began fighting, I knew we would be victorious due to your unwavering devotion and courage. Such cannot lose. There will be other battles in the future, but for now, peace will reign in our land. There was rejoicing last night while you served the wounded. Tonight let the real festivities begin. We have much to be thankful for, and the King loves it when His people celebrate together."

King Ronan walked with Arden and Zoe to the tables where the food was placed. They ate a delightful meal that had been prepared as a victory dinner. When they finished, King Ronan wanted to speak with Arden and Zoe.

"Zoe, you are a very courageous young lady. You fought like a true warrior. You were the one the King used to turn the tide of battle and break the will of the enemy. No wonder the enemy has been after you so intently on your journey. I suppose it was Feena who taught you how to shoot like that. Such archery is rare even among the elves."

"Thank you, King Ronan. Yes, she was my instructor, but also my friend. I love her dearly and was sorry that we could not visit longer. She, Bantry, Antrum, and some other close friends had to leave quickly to confront a new pack of wolves that Evan spotted in Hemlock Forest."

"Feena will be fine, Zoe, and we will send her help though she never really needs it. She has lived in that forest for years and is most revered by those who live there. Those wolves will soon come to respect her wisdom and skills, and then they will leave her alone."

King Ronan seemed to be studying Zoe. "I can see why my son is so smitten by you. You are quite beautiful and you have a good and kind heart. I saw what you did for Kavian, and it was nothing short of a miracle. You are a wonderful girl and, if it is the King's will, I will be pleased and honored for you to marry my son and become my daughter."

Zoe's eyes widened. "Oh, thank you King Ronan. You are too kind." She looked at Arden, but did not have the heart to say she was not certain about marrying him. "Arden is quite a special young man, from a very special family."

"Zoe, after our victory celebration, there is a tent prepared for you under the huge oak tree by the river. I pray that you sleep well tonight my dear—you certainly deserve to rest." King Ronan bowed and then walked toward the festivities.

Arden grabbed Zoe's hand. "You said nothing about us, Zoe. Why?"

She shrugged her shoulders and grinned. "Maybe he is correct in his assumption...and I hope he is right."

Arden's eyes widened with surprise. "Do you mean that?"

"We shall see Arden."

"I love you Zoe—that will never change."

"Thank you Arden."

They spent the evening celebrating their victory, with singing, dancing, and great merriment.

✦═ ❋ ═✦

The sun cast long shadows in the forest as Zoe awoke and breathed in the fresh morning air. It was early, but she had slept well and was ready to begin her journey once again. She walked outside the tent and found Brogan and Kavian fast asleep. "Wake up—it's time to rise and shine!" She gently shook both of them and they sleepily opened their eyes.

Kavian yawned. "It's morning already?"

"Yes—we must eat breakfast. Don't you smell the ham and eggs cooking?"

"Now that you mention it, I do."

While they were eating, Zoe asked Arden, "Will you keep Dapple here for me? The mountains are not far and I think it will be too difficult for her to climb them."

Arden placed his hands in Zoe's. "She will be waiting here when you return."

They finished eating breakfast and walked to Zoe's tent. "Arden, I must leave now while the day is still early, I am so anxious to continue on."

Arden brushed his hand across her cheek. "I will be praying for you throughout the remainder of your journey—of that you can be sure."

Zoe quickly packed her things and told all of her new friends goodbye. Mahon saw that Zoe was leaving and prayed for a safe journey and then blessed her. "Go my child." He looked deeply into her eyes. "There is a life-changing surprise that awaits you. You will not like this surprise at first, but you must trust the King and then you will know just how much He loves you."

Zoe seemed puzzled. "How do you know this Mahon?"

"The King revealed it to me. Just remember to trust the King— no matter what happens."

Arden walked with her to the path. "Zoe, I know the King will watch over you." He touched her silky brown hair. "The sooner you leave, my love, the sooner we will be reunited." He drew her into his arms and then kissed her on the cheek. "Goodbye, my warrior Princess."

"Farewell, Arden. Thank you for understanding how I feel. I do hope to see you soon, too." She blew him a kiss and then once again began walking on her chosen path with Kavian and Brogan.

As we walk bravely forward,
His light will guide the way.

Part VI
The
Journey Continues

Chapter Twenty-Four

But we proved to be gentle among you, as a nursing mother
tenderly cares for her own children.
I Thessalonians 2:7

The path took a turn and began to wind around a pasture where the tall grass swirled wildly in the wind. A dozen brown and white horses were grazing in the field to their left. Zoe's attention quickly changed when she saw Brogan running ahead.

"Come back, Brogan!"

He did not answer. Zoe and Kavian ran after him, but could not keep up. As they ran around the curve in the path, they saw him in the distance sitting in the road. Breathless, Zoe finally reached him. "What are you doing?" Her eyes wandered. "My goodness, you've found a little girl!" Zoe immediately noticed her big green eyes and the thick blond hair that fell to her waist in curls. She could not be more than five years old.

"Sorry I didn't have time to tell you, but I knew I needed to get to her."

The little girl stood back and stared at Brogan. "You talk!"

"Yes, I do. What do you think about that?"

A smile played at the corners of her mouth. "I have never heard a wolf talk before...I like you." She began patting his head.

Then Kavian spoke. "Hello there. I talk too!"

She walked over to Kavian and patted his head. Zoe bent down so she could be eye level with the child. "What's your name?"

"Faith."

"What a pretty name! Do you live near here?"

"I think so."

"Were you with someone today—maybe your mother or father?"

Faith's chin began to quiver. "Yes, I was with my mother," she whimpered.

Zoe picked up Faith and held her. "Everything is going to be fine. Do you know where your mother is?"

Sniffing, Faith explained. "No, we were outside and she told me to stay by the cottage while she went to find some sticks. She was going to start a fire and cook, but it took her a long time." She hiccupped. "I saw a butterfly and chased it for a while. Then I couldn't find our cottage. I walked and walked."

Zoe hugged Faith. "We'll help you find your mother."

"Brogan and Kavian, what do you think is the best way to do this?"

Brogan spoke first. "I think you and Faith should stay here. I have a good scent of Faith so I should be able to find her home or mother soon."

Kavian added, "Brogan, you go north and I'll go south. We'll cover more territory that way. Zoe and Faith, you stay right here and don't move. We'll be back as soon as we can."

"Good plan. We'll stay here and wait for you." Brogan and Kavian ran off sniffing the air as they left.

Faith sobbed, "I want my mother."

"I know you do, little one. Are you hungry?" She nodded. "Let me see what I have in my bag." King Ronan's servants had packed them plenty of food. "I have cheese, bread, grapes, and even some sweet cakes. Here, sit down on this big rock and we'll eat." Faith hungrily ate the food and asked for more. Zoe gave her a few more grapes and then she seem satisfied.

"How old are you Faith?"

"I just turned five years old. My mother says I'm more like ten because I talk so well for my age," Her whole face lit up in a smile.

"Well, you do talk like a big girl and I'm sure we'll find your mother soon."

"I hope so because I miss her. She's very nice." Faith sleepily yawned and Zoe found herself doing likewise.

She brushed Faith's hair off her face. "Would you like for me to tell you a story that I learned as a little girl?"

"Oh yes, I love stories."

Zoe smiled. "Once upon a time there was a little girl with hair as golden as the sun and eyes as green as emeralds."

"That sounds like me—I have golden hair and green eyes!"

"Yes you do."

"As the story goes, she lived in a tiny little cottage with her sick mother and three cats. They were very poor and did not have much to eat, so every day the little girl would go to the brook and catch fish for her cats and mother to eat. Then one day, she caught a very large fish and in its mouth was a huge nugget of gold. The fish said, 'If you will let me go free, you may have this gold.' The little girl agreed and then ran to her little home to show her mother the gold. Her mother was very happy for she knew the gold was worth much. They sold the gold and her mother was able to buy medicine to be healed. They were never poor again, and they lived happily ever after."

"I like that story!"

"It was my favorite story as a child. My mother used to tell it to me all the time." Zoe found her eyes misting with tears.

"Are you crying, Zoe?"

"Oh I'm okay. Here, let's move over by this tree and sit down while I sing you a song."

Faith plopped down on Zoe's lap and she rocked her back and forth while singing a sweet melody that relaxed and soothed Faith to sleep. Soon after, Zoe leaned against the tree and closed her eyes.

It seemed as if they had just fallen asleep when Brogan abruptly woke them. "I found her!"

Zoe yawned. "Who?"

"Faith's mother!"

Before she could reply, Faith was already running into her mother's arms. Her mother grabbed her and held her tight. "Oh,

Faith, you're safe. Thank the King! I've been searching everywhere for you!"

"I missed you, Mother."

"I missed you too, Faith, but why did you leave? Remember, I told you to stay beside the cottage while I searched for wood."

"I know—I'm sorry. I saw a butterfly and chased it and then I was lost."

Soon Kavian returned. "I see you've found her. Good work, Brogan!"

Jenna did not notice Kavian for she was talking with Faith. She cupped her little face in her hands and said, "You must obey me, Faith. What if someone had not helped you? I have told you many times that there are wild animals in the forest. I am just thankful you are safe." She hugged her once more.

"I won't do it again."

"I will trust that you will always obey me, Faith." Jenna's eyes wandered to Zoe. "In all the excitement I forgot to introduce myself. My name is Jenna."

Zoe smiled, "I'm pleased to meet you. I'm Zoe, and of course you know Brogan."

"Yes, you cannot imagine my surprise when he spoke!"

"He is special." Zoe knelt down to pat him on the head. "And he's the best friend anyone could ever have, along with Kavian of course." She patted him on the head, as well.

Jenna stepped back with Faith. Zoe quickly spoke up. "He's very friendly like Brogan. Don't let his size scare you. He's a follower of the King, too."

"Nice to meet you too, Kavian."

Kavian bowed. "The pleasure is mine."

"I don't know how to thank you enough. I'll never forget your kindness to my daughter. My cottage is very close and it's going to be dark soon. Would you please join us for supper and stay the night?"

Zoe, Brogan, and Kavian answered, "Yes," at the same time. They all laughed.

"Well, let's head home then." Faith played with Brogan and Kavian as they walked. Endlessly Faith would throw a stick to each of them and they would return, ready to do it all over again.

As they were walking along, Zoe noticed something glowing in the sun by a rock. She bent down and picked it up and discovered that it was another key, which was inscribed, *GENTLENESS*. She fingered the key for a moment, and then placed it in her pocket. Gentleness began to flow deeply within. She had always longed to be of a gentle spirit, and now with a thankful heart the key was already becoming deeply rooted.

The key to gentleness is kindness mixed with tenderness and compassion.

Chapter Twenty-Five

*...I will turn their mourning into joy, and will comfort them,
and give them joy for their sorrow.
Jeremiah 31:13*

"Have you lived in this area long, Jenna?"

"About seven years ago we moved here when Phillip and I were first married. We were so happy until about two years ago when Phillip died. It has been difficult for Faith and me ever since then—in so many ways. But somehow we've managed."

Zoe watched as tears filled Jenna's dark blue eyes. Jenna wiped the tears as though she was trying to wipe the pain from her heart.

"I am so sorry, Jenna."

"Thank you, but at least I have Faith. When I look at her, I see Phillip. She has his deep-set green eyes and smile. He was a wonderful husband, a good provider, and father. One day he was here and the next he was gone. He was outside gathering firewood and a snake bit him. He ran into the house and told me what had happened. He said he felt sick and was going to lie down. I didn't know what to do for him! He soon had chills, fever, and then became delirious. He died that evening—he was gone that quickly!" Jenna relived the pain as though it had just happened.

Zoe hugged her and tried to comfort her. Before long Jenna's home was in sight, right on Zoe's chosen path. They had only walked a mile from where they had found Faith. As Zoe approached the little cottage, she saw it was stone just like hers, and was surrounded with purple, yellow, and pink wildflowers. She heard a stream in the back and they walked around to see it. As Zoe knelt down and drank from the cool water, she thought of her own little cottage.

"Phillip thought of everything when we built this cottage. To have clean water so close to our home has been a blessing."

"He must have been a wise man." Zoe looked around the area. "You must work very hard in your garden for your flowers to be this beautiful."

"Flowers are my hobby now, but they are not nearly as pretty as they were when Phillip was alive. It was his joy to see the glorious color of the flowers decorating our yard. I have often wished that I had worked alongside him more often so I could have learned the secrets he surely possessed in gardening. Well, enough about that. It's beginning to get cool so we should go inside."

As they walked in, the first thing that caught Zoe's attention was the huge stone fireplace. She could just imagine the fire glow radiating its warmth inside the little cottage. Flowers were in vases everywhere, filling the air with their sweet fragrance. There were two big beds at one end of the cottage near two, curtained, small windows, which added to the homey feeling.

"Faith and I can share a bed tonight. Zoe, you can sleep on this one. Brogan and Kavian, I will place two nice thick blankets in front of the fireplace so you will be snug and warm tonight while you sleep."

"We'll enjoy that," Brogan replied, and Kavian nodded.

Jenna told them to sit down and make themselves comfortable while she prepared dinner. Before long it was ready.

"Everything is delicious, Jenna. You're a very fine cook," Zoe said. Jenna nodded her thanks with pleasure.

After everyone was full, they cleaned up and then sat down in front of the warm fire ready to enjoy the evening together. But it was not long before, Faith, Kavian, and Brogan were lulled to sleep by the cozy warmth. Zoe decided it was a good time to ask Jenna a question she had been thinking about all afternoon.

"I don't mean to be prying, but I was wondering—do you know the King?"

Jenna thought about an experience she had had years ago. "When I was a little girl, my mother told me about the King. I believe my mother must have known Him because she talked about Him all the time. I often thought I would like to know Him myself. I believe Phillip knew Him too, but from a distance. He occasionally talked about the King, and as he was dying, he called out to Him."

"Jenna, last spring I received an invitation to go the King's house in Remiah. Recently, I met Him and He is more wonderful than I could ever imagine."

Jenna looked thoughtful. "I have been feeling like something is missing in my life—I was not certain what it was until you mentioned the King's name. Is it possible for me to go on this journey too?"

"Of course. Before I received His invitation, I was not certain Remiah existed, or even the King for that matter—I had heard about Him, but that was all. Now I know He is real."

"Even if I asked the King to go to Remiah and was invited, how could I travel with Faith?"

"I think every journey is different. The road you take will not be the same as mine. The King knows your life completely and He will choose the right path for you and one that He knows you can follow. I have thought about this many times. Every journey is different because each of us are so different. I believe He will teach you all you need to know on whatever path He leads you. He would never deny anyone who wants to know Him better. Why not ask Him for an invitation and see what happens?"

Jenna seemed excited "I believe I will!"

"Jenna, when I saw the King recently, He gave me His Book of Words. Let me get it and find a verse I think will help you." Zoe hastily thumbed through the pages. "Oh, yes, here it is:"

Draw near to God and He will draw near to you (James 4:8).

Jenna smiled knowing exactly what the verse meant. "I will do that."

Zoe yawned, "This has been a good day, Jenna."

"Yes, it has. I have much to think about. Thank you for talking to me, Zoe." She leaned over and hugged her. "Would you mind if I read the King's Book for a little while?"

"Why, certainly you can. I will put Faith to bed for you."

"How thoughtful of you. I know how special this Book is to you so I will take good care of it."

Zoe smiled and touched her on her shoulder. "Goodnight, Jenna."

Long after everyone was asleep, Jenna continued to read the King's Book well into the night. She found comfort and love in His Words—just what she needed. She made a decision in her heart that she wanted to follow the King from now on. It had been a long time since she felt peace and joy in her heart, and never to the extent she felt it at this moment—it was a good feeling.

When the light was just barely shining in the window, Zoe awoke and saw that everyone was still sound asleep. She quietly got up and added more wood to the dying embers of the fire, and soon it was blazing again. Brogan and Kavian stirred so she let them outside. She saw the King's Book sitting on the table so she picked it up and began reading. How truly awesome the King is— the more she read, the more she realized that she could turn to His Book and find guidance for any problem, comfort for any sadness, as well as read a love story, poetry, wisdom, and most importantly read about the great love He has for all of His people. Truly His Words are to be treasured above all.

Last evening when she talked to Jenna about the King, Zoe knew her joy was found in the King. He had truly captured her heart. Starting today, she would live that way. She took out her journal and wrote about the many things that had recently happened in her life—Kavian's redemption, Arden, the war, Jenna and Faith, and much more. This had been a wonderful journey. Her mind wandered to what Mahon had said about something happening on her journey that would be life-changing—everything has been life changing! The King had said this would be her greatest test.

She laid those thoughts aside for she knew Jenna and Faith would be getting up soon and she wanted to start breakfast. As she closed her journal and placed it in her bag, a key fell out. She picked it up and saw that it was inscribed, *JOY.* She placed it in her pocket and immediately felt joy bubbling deep within. She found herself smiling and then laughing because she was so happy. She would treasure this key always because it marked the day that she had truly discovered that the greatest joy of all comes from having a close relationship with the King.

The key to joy is found in following HIM.

Chapter Twenty-Six

Let all that you do be done in love.
I Corinthians 16:14

The sunlight cast a golden glow in the cabin as Zoe was busily preparing breakfast. Jenna could not remember the last time someone had prepared a meal for her. "It smells wonderful Zoe. What are you cooking?"

"Scones and eggs with cheese."

"Thank you so much!"

"You are quite welcome."

Zoe hummed as she put breakfast on the table. While they were eating, Zoe told Jenna about some of the adventures she had experienced on her journey. Jenna was amazed. "You certainly are brave, Zoe. I don't think I could have ever fought in a war!"

"I have learned to do many things that I never thought I would be able to do. It's amazing what you can do when you have to!"

"I suppose you are right about that."

Jenna told Zoe that she had determined to follow the King, and that she at last felt peace and joy in her life.

"Jenna, I'm so happy for you and I will be praying for you. You and Faith are going to be just fine now. I wish we could stay longer, but we really do need to be going. It is still early and I am so anxious to go to Remiah. Arden, a friend of mine, told me we are very close."

Jenna seemed stunned. "I'm amazed. I've been close to Remiah all of my life and didn't know it! I understand that you have to go, but we'll miss you. Oh, I packed a sack of food for your journey that should last several days."

"How kind of you! Thank you so much Jenna."

"I'm sincerely grateful to you all for finding Faith yesterday. And Zoe, thank you so much for talking to me last night. My life will never be the same. Please, come see us anytime. We will miss you all."

Faith hugged Brogan and Kavian and began crying. "Mommy, I have never had a dog. I know Brogan is Zoe's friend, but what about Kavian? Does he have a family?"

Jenna did not know what to say. Zoe spoke something in Kavian's ear. "Faith, wait here. I need to talk to Kavian."

Zoe could not believe she was even thinking this way—as hard as it would be. But in her heart, she knew it was right. "Kavian, what do you think? Do you want to stay here with Jenna and Faith?"

"Zoe, I promised I would guard you with my life. I gave you my word."

"I know Kavian, and you have—but what would you like to do?"

"I've never had a friend like you Zoe, and now that I have learned that Brogan is my son, I feel torn between staying with you two and being with Jenna and Faith. But somehow I feel these two need me more than you do right now. I could protect them in the forest and play with Faith. But what do you think I should do?"

"I think you are the most honorable friend anyone could ever have," she winked at Brogan, "besides Brogan of course. As much as we'll miss you, I think it's right for you to stay with them. We will visit soon though—you have found a special place in my heart and I love you Kavian."

"Thank you Zoe. You're the first true friend I've ever had, and I will never forget your kindness."

Kavian realized that he needed to talk to Brogan about this too.

"What do you think Brogan?"

"As hard as it will be to part with you, especially now that I know you're my father, and as much as I will miss you, I think this is what you're supposed to do. But as Zoe said, we must plan to visit soon."

"You can count on that, Brogan."

They walked back to where Faith and Jenna were standing. Zoe touched Jenna on the arm. "Could I talk to you?"

"What do you think about Kavian staying with you and Faith?"

Jenna did not have to think about it very long. "I think it would be wonderful. Both of us think he is very special! Faith would be thrilled, but we would not want to take him from you."

"Kavian believes he should stay. We'll miss him terribly, but I think this is where he belongs. He will guard you with his life. You are close to the kingdom, but just being close to the kingdom can be a dangerous place. This is where most of the snakes gather to attack the sojourners."

They walked back to the group. Zoe bent down to talk to Faith. "How would you like for Kavian to stay with you and your mother and be your friend?"

Faith nearly knocked Kavian down with a hug. Zoe laughed. "I'll take that as a yes!"

Zoe leaned down and touched Kavian on his head, "I truly believe we will see each other again, but if for some reason our paths do not cross, I'll never forget you Kavian." A tear slid down Zoe's cheek. "You have been a dear friend."

"Thank you Zoe. You not only saved my life, you led me to true life. I will forever serve the King who has done so much for me, and I will do whatever He asks of me. I know that staying with Jenna and Faith is His will, and I rejoice in His purpose for me. Even so, I will miss you, and hope I have the chance to serve you again too."

Kavian frolicked with Brogan until Zoe said it was time to leave. Everyone hugged and said their goodbyes. Kavian sat down beside Faith and licked her face, and she giggled. Jenna and Faith were just what Kavian needed, and likewise they needed him too. But, oh, how she was going to miss him! She hugged him one last time, turned back to wave, and then left.

Zoe was crying, but she did not want Kavian to see, so she did not turn around again. "So this is the result of loving your enemy! He was my worst enemy and now I could not love him more!"

To be selfless is placing other's needs above our own—the highest act of kindness.

Chapter Twenty-Seven

..."How often shall my brother sin against me,
and I forgive him? Up to seven times?
..."I do not say to you, up to seven times, but up to
seventy times seven."
Matthew 18:21-22 (NKJV)

Zoe was deep in thought about Kavian when Brogan spoke. "That was a wonderful thing you did letting Kavian stay with Jenna and Faith. Kavian has a special place in your heart, as he does mine, but you put the needs of Jenna and Faith above your own. I am proud to be your companion. I know I can trust you to always do the right thing. Not everyone has the opportunity to serve someone like you."

"Thank you Brogan. I was thinking this morning about how nice it would be if they had a dog, but I guess I didn't think about Kavian. It was right for him to stay. We will miss him, though."

"We will that, and now it is just us again. I'm so glad to have found my father, and I believe we will see each other before too long. In fact, I know we will be together, but I also know that we need this time apart to grow. When I see him again we're going to be a real father and son. It's truly a remarkable thing the way the King ordered our paths to meet the way we did."

Zoe looked at Brogan with amazement. "You are certainly wise beyond your age!"

After they had walked a short time, Zoe saw their final destination, just ahead. "Look Brogan! The mountains—I see the mountains in the distance! Come on, we must walk faster!"

Brogan was glad to oblige. Soon he ran way ahead of Zoe. She yelled breathlessly, "You don't need to run that fast!" He slowed down and finally she caught up with him.

In the distance, she noticed someone approaching them from another path. It was a woman, and Zoe had the feeling that she had seen her somewhere before. It was hard to tell but she looked to be in her thirties or forties. She had chestnut hair that fell to the middle of her back, and was very thin and frail looking. Zoe stared trying to place her.

When they at last came close enough to speak, Zoe gave the woman a reassuring smile, but the strange feeling that she had seen her before would not leave. "Hello, beautiful day, is it not?"

The woman responded. "Yes, it is."

Zoe could not shake the apprehension she felt. *Where is that coming from?* "Are you traveling alone?"

"Yes, I am." The woman said sitting on a nearby rock.

Intrigued with the woman, Zoe asked, "Brogan and I were just going to stop and eat. Would you care to join us?"

The woman quickly accepted. "Oh, yes, I would like that," she said with a grateful look.

With Jenna's food, and what Arden had sent, Zoe had a wide variety to offer the woman. "We have cheese scones, apples—"

"Oh that is just fine."

"But there is more to choose from."

"Cheese scones and apples sound delicious."

"Certainly." Brogan came and sat down beside Zoe, having been instructed by her in the past not to talk to strangers unless she introduced him.

While they were eating, they talked about trivial things like the weather until Zoe changed the subject. "Please excuse my manners. We have been sitting here eating, and I have not even introduced myself. My name is Zoe Newbridge."

All the color drained from the woman's face. She dropped her apple and whispered, "What did you say your name was?"

Zoe replied very slowly, "Zoe Newbridge."

Her voice was broken with emotion and she could barely speak. "I kept looking at you thinking that it just might be you! Zoe, I am Mary Newbridge, your mother!"

Zoe sat very still. She fought her feelings, but could not stop the bitterness and hatred that was rising up from deep within. She looked at her coldly, stood up, and began packing her belongings.

"Zoe, please do not go!"

"You show up now, after all these years! You left me when I was four years old with my aunt and cousins! How could you? I used to dream of the day when you would return for me and take me home, but you never came!" Sobbing, Zoe said, "I'm on my own now—I'm doing just fine and I don't need you!"

She grabbed her things and began walking in the opposite direction of her chosen road.

Brogan called to her, "Wait, Zoe!"

Zoe ran aimlessly, not caring where she went. She thought her mother must have been sent by the enemy to stop her from finishing her journey. Here she was, almost to Remiah and her mother shows up! Blinding tears plummeted down Zoe's face as she ran. She finally stopped, wiped her tears, and looked around realizing she was lost.

Brogan caught up with her. "Why did you do that? You should not have run away. Just recently you were telling Kavian and me about your mother and how you needed to forgive her. Now is your chance! You need to talk to her Zoe. Go back to her!"

"No, I cannot do it. I will not do it! I don't want to see her. She is the cause of most of the pain in my life. Why should I want to be with her now?"

"She is your mother. When the King visited us, He said you were going to face your most difficult test. Do you remember what Mahon said? Something life-changing was going to happen, and you would not like it at first. You know this is it, Zoe."

"How can I forgive my mother? She deserted me when I needed her the most!"

Brogan sat down next to her. "Zoe, think about Kavian. He was your greatest enemy and mine, and now we both love him so much. That is why your paths have met again. How can you ever completely love until you have forgiven and love the one who hurt you the most?"

"Brogan, I understand what you're saying. But it is not that simple! She did a terrible thing to me and it's not going to be easy to forgive her—if ever I could."

"You said you wanted to be free from the rejection that you felt from your mother. By going back and forgiving her, you will begin to be healed, and so will she."

"I don't want to face her…I'm afraid to face her. I remember a sweet, kind mother, and th—then she left me," she sobbed. "Why would she come back now?"

Hopelessness flooded Zoe's soul. *This is the test—anything but this!* She sat a long time thinking about what she should do. She threw rocks while her mind raced. Reluctantly, Zoe stood up. As difficult as it would be, she knew what she had to do.

"I'm ready to go." They walked silently. At last she saw the road—and finally, far in the distance she saw her mother. *Please dear King—help me! I don't know what to do or say.*

She approached her mother, who was still sitting on the rock. She looked devastated. With relief, Mary saw Zoe. "I know you must hate me and I don't blame you. I probably would have run off too. But please, let me try to explain why I left so long ago."

Zoe sat down beside her mother.

"When I gave birth to you, I had no husband. As you know, when this happens, unwed mothers are shunned by others, and by almost everyone except the ones you never want to come near your children. Your father didn't want to marry me. I had shamed my parents and they refused to help me. So at the age of fifteen, I was on my own. I decided to move to Brenlough to be near my sister. She was the only one who had any sympathy for my situation. She took care of you during the day while I worked. But then a wonderful thing happened. I found a job cooking for a wealthy family in the village. We were able to get our own little cottage and we had so much fun together.

"But one day they told me they no longer needed my services. I became so depressed that I was no longer taking good care of you. So I left you with my sister and her children, thinking you would be better off without me.

"I tried to build a new life for myself, so I could return for you. You were all I loved in this life, and the hope that I would one day see you again is what has kept me alive. I just never could get on my feet again so I could return for you. As the years went by, I tried to tell myself you were happy and better off. I knew I was wrong leaving you—I should have at least visited you, but I felt too guilty for what I had done. I also felt that if people knew you were mine I would only bring you shame. I began to carry a weight of guilt that was just too heavy to bear, but I didn't know what else to do. Recently though, things began to look up for me and I began a journey, which I will explain later. I cannot help but believe that we were meant to run into each other like this. I know you may not understand Zoe, and I'm so sorry for the pain I've caused in your life. Please forgive me."

Zoe's mind was racing with many thoughts. Mary paused. "I understand if you feel you can't forgive me, but I will always treasure these few moments with you forever." Mary looked like she was trying to memorize every feature on Zoe's face. "All the hardships of my journey were worth just seeing you again. You are more beautiful than I ever dreamed."

Zoe listened, and could not help but begin to soften. Even so, there was a lot of bitterness and hardness to get over—too much to just give up in a few moments. "I can see you had a really hard life, and I'm sorry for that. I just wish I could have had my mother while I was growing up. You hurt me deeply and I feel like I lost so much."

"Zoe, I'm deeply sorry for the pain I've caused you. I just wish I could make everything right. I knew it was too much to expect...I suppose it was not realistic for me to think you would accept me back. I now realize how foolish I was to think that. You're right Zoe. It is too much for me to expect you to forgive me."

They sat in silence for a long time. Brogan put his paw on Zoe's knee. She knew what he was thinking—that she needed to forgive her. *How can I? I cannot force myself to forgive her.*

Zoe stood up. "Would you mind if I took a walk?"

"Of course not..."

Brogan and Zoe walked for a while before either spoke. Brogan began, "What are you thinking about?"

"The King was right—this is the most difficult test of my journey. I don't know how to forgive her!"

"At least you're taking a step toward forgiving her, I mean by trying. Why is it so hard to forgive her? You forgave Kavian."

"I think because I've had so many years to build up pain and bitterness in my heart for her that it's hard to let that go."

"What did you see when you looked in your mother's eyes?"

"Sadness, pain, guilt..."

"Do you think she is sincere then—I mean about being sorry for everything?"

"I suppose so."

Brogan looked deeply in Zoe's eyes, "I was just thinking about how many times the King has forgiven us."

"So you're saying because He forgives us, I should forgive her?"

"Yes, that is exactly what I'm saying."

"Look how many times we made mistakes on this journey, yet the King always forgave and continued to help us many times."

Zoe sighed. "I need to think." She sat down under the shade of a willow tree. Brogan laid down and dozed. Zoe opened the King's Book and read for a long time. She came upon a verse that confirmed what Brogan had just said to her.

"And whenever you stand praying, forgive, if you have anything against anyone; so that your Father also who is in heaven may forgive you your transgressions."
Mark 11:25

Zoe closed the Book and sighed. "Oh dear King, give me strength to do what seems so impossible."

Forgiveness cleanses us of bitterness, resentment, and pain.

Chapter Twenty-Eight

*And if I have the gift of prophecy, and know all mysteries and all
knowledge; and if I have all faith, so as to remove mountains,
but do not have love, I am nothing.*
I Corinthians 13:2

Zoe sat under the frail leaves of the willow tree, which swayed
with the wind, back and forth, just like her mind seemed
to be doing. How could she truly forgive her mother if the
hurt was so deep within? But she also realized that all she had
learned on her journey would be worth nothing if she could
not forgive her—the King had forgiven her numerous times and
continued to love her unconditionally.

With resolution, she stood up. "Wake up Brogan—we have to go."

Sleepily, Brogan stood, yawned, and walked slowly beside Zoe.
"What's on your mind, Zoe?"

"Many, many things, Brogan." He did not ask her any more for
he could see she was deep in thought.

Soon they were back where they had left Mary. She was sitting
with her head looking down. Zoe stood behind a bush and watched
her for a few minutes. There was a sadness that seemed to be the
essence of Mary. The frown lines on her forehead revealed that
she had worried much in her life. When Mary lifted her head, Zoe
detected a lifeless look in her eyes—disclosing that life had not
been happy for her. But it was the droop of her shoulders and
tears silently flowing down her cheeks that seemed to soften
Zoe's heart the most toward her mother. As Zoe stared at her, she
realized that maybe she had judged her mother too harshly. Even
though she was still hurt, she was not the only one who had a
hard life. Her mother had no husband, but still tried to raise her,

and then when she felt she had no choice but to leave her with her sister, lived with tormenting guilt for all these years. That she would now have the courage to try and make things right revealed a deep commitment and strength left in her mother's character.

Mary glanced up and saw Zoe. "You're back! I was beginning to think you had decided to leave."

"I just needed some time to think things over and I made a discovery. Please listen and I will tell you exactly how I feel, and we can go on from there."

Zoe began pacing back and forth and cleared her throat. Then with resolve, she stopped and intently gazed at her mother. "For all these years, I never thought about what you were going through, only about *me*—what a difficult time I was having. I suppose there really are two sides to every story. When you abandoned me and didn't return, I believed you did not love me, which was hard for a four-year-old to handle. I have thought my whole life that there was something deeply wrong with me."

Zoe's thoughts wandered away. "A Prince fell in love with me, and I could not even love him back for fear he would abandon me when he found out what was wrong with me. I know it sounds silly, but I just could not shake this deep feeling that I am not really lovable..."

Tears were streaming down Mary's face. "I'm so, so sorry! When your father wouldn't marry me, when I was pregnant with you, I felt the same way. Since then I have never been able to love anyone on earth but you."

Zoe looked at her mother and could not help but to melt a little more. She continued "As I think about my life, I realize that I always had someone watching over me—the King! Every part of my life has taken me one step closer to Him. The greatest King of all actually loves me! And now, I feel Him pushing me toward you. He actually loves you too. What I'm attempting to say is that I forgive you. I'll no longer hold what has happened in the past against you. I realize now that everything that has happened has somehow been for our good."

Mary was now sobbing as she walked to Zoe and held out her arms to her. Zoe was hesitant at first but then stepped forward and allowed her mother to embrace her. Before long she began to feel her heart soften even more toward Mary and she genuinely hugged her back. They hugged for a long time. And then the impossible happened—the years of rejection that Zoe had felt melted away, and the years of guilt that Mary had suffered were lifted from her. Their hug was a bond of love. Now Zoe knew she had truly forgiven her mother, and where hatred, bitterness, and an abandoned heart had been, love could now grow.

Zoe stepped back and looked at her mother. She could not believe she was truly standing right in front of her. She smiled and Mary returned the smile revealing a depth of beauty that Zoe had not seen before. She touched her mother's cheek, "Well, I guess you did come back for me after all! What a day this has been!"

Mary smiled with new life in her eyes. "What a *wonderful* day this has been—more wonderful than I could have ever dreamed. You are not only the most beautiful young lady I have ever seen, you are the most gracious. You are a true Princess!"

Mary could not interpret the look she saw on Zoe's face as she suddenly gazed far away into the distance. "If only you knew the whole story!"

"Well, it seems important. I would like to know."

Zoe smiled, "And I will tell you very soon."

Brogan stood at a distance and heard everything. He walked up to Zoe wondering if it was the right time to come.

"Oh, I'm sorry, Brogan." She turned to her mother. "I want to introduce Brogan to you—my best friend."

Mary knelt down and patted Brogan on the head. "I am most pleased to meet you."

"And I am *so* glad to meet you!"

Mary turned pale. "He just spoke Zoe!"

"I suppose I should have told you that first," she giggled. "The King gave him the gift of speech."

"My goodness…this is a wonder of wonders! Now I am wondering if I am really in a dream!" Mary replied.

Brogan spoke up. "I don't mean to interrupt this joyous occasion, but it's already dark, and I noticed a cave very close to the road—a few hundred feet from here. It would make a good place to stay for the night."

"Good, Brogan. Let's go."

Zoe helped her mother gather her belongings and then they walked to the cave and settled in for the night. Zoe made a fire outside the cave to help warm them. They ate and then talked for hours, attempting to catch up on each other's lives. Zoe listened intently as her mother spoke, hardly believing she was truly with her.

"Zoe, you are so beautiful. I am amazed that you have not married. Your heart is so kind, and you walk with grace and confidence—like true royalty. I am thankful for the fine job my sister did to raise such a special young woman. I am not just feeling sorry for myself by saying this, but perhaps you were better off living with a family, rather than an unwed mother."

"Well, I always wished you were with me, but we cannot change what happened in the past, so let's just move on."

"You're right Zoe. You are a very wise young lady."

"Thank you. You look so tired. I think it might be best if you rested. I do have something to tell you though—there is a man—actually a Prince, who I mentioned earlier who is interested in me."

"I must say I am anxious to hear all about this young man. How can I sleep when for so many years I dreamed of having this conversation with my daughter, and now, like a dream from heaven, it's happening. Please go on and tell me."

"Mother, I too have dreamed of this conversation with you. And one thing you can be sure—it is a dream from heaven that has come true. Even so, I want to tell you all about him when we are fresh. Tomorrow we will have plenty of time to talk, but for now we need to get some sleep."

Brogan and Mary fell asleep almost immediately on their mats. Zoe lay awake for a long time, even as tired as she was. She had too much on her mind. She went outside and put some more sticks on the fire, took out her journal, and wrote about this extraordinary day. When she finished, she thanked the King for giving her a second chance to know and love her mother, and the strength to do what she felt was impossible. She looked at her mother and thought. *She is even more wonderful than I had dared to dream. This test was truly the best of all!*

Zoe saw something glowing in a bush. She walked over to it and saw a large gold key ring hanging on a limb. She picked it up and was surprised to feel how heavy it was. Inscribed on the ring was the word *LOVE.* She immediately took all of the keys out of her pocket and put them on the key ring one by one. Now she understood the verse she had read so recently:

LOVE NEVER FAILS! (I Corinthians 13:8)

Just like the key ring is round and does not have a beginning or end, love is constant and unconditional—it never fails. She understood at once why *LOVE* was a key ring and not a key. Love is the bond that holds the other keys together. It is the most powerful force on earth because it brought heaven to earth.

Then she thought about each key that she had received: *PEACE, FAITHFULNESS, PATIENCE, GOODNESS, SELF-CONTROL, KINDNESS, GENTLENESS, JOY,* and now the key ring, *LOVE,* the force behind all the keys. These keys were just seeds in her heart, but she knew they could never have grown to their full potential without love.

When Zoe placed the keys on the key ring and then put them back in her pocket, she felt love burn deeply inside. It was quite painful at first, but then slowly the pain left, and love melted within the depths of her soul. This had been the hardest key of all to receive, but by far the most important. The heaviness of the key ring was now gone, and seemed to become part of her, even though she could plainly see it in her pocket. Love was but a tiny seed growing in her heart, but with care, this love would grow into a deep love.

She went inside the cave and snuggled underneath her blankets. She glanced over at her mother and saw she was still sleeping peacefully. She looked so tranquil, content, and fulfilled— and now Zoe could rest too.

The key to love is forgiveness,
and likewise the key to forgiveness is love.

Part VII
The
Journey's End

Chapter Twenty-Nine

*I press on toward the goal for the prize of the
upward call of God in Christ Jesus.*
Philippians 3:14

Zoe and Mary spent several days getting to know each other, often laughing and crying at the same time. Zoe found herself growing closer and closer to her mother. She discovered that in many ways she was one of the most remarkable women she had ever met. She also knew that there was probably no one who had ever seen this in Mary before. Then she heard the King's voice within her so loudly as if He were speaking to her audibly, "I have always seen the remarkable woman that your mother is. She is a Princess too."

She wondered how many people are such treasures, and no one ever notices.

While Mary was picking berries, Zoe decided to study the map. All she had to do was climb a mountain in the range that was right across the valley from them. Remiah was at the top. She had already been through so much—it was hard to believe that it was this close.

Mary picked a whole bag of ripe berries and came to show them to Zoe when she found her deep in thought. "What are you doing, Zoe?"

"I am studying this map. I have not told you yet, but I'm on my way to see the King. He lives on top of the highest mountain in the distance—a place called Remiah. Have you ever heard of the King?"

Mary smiled. "Well, yes I have. In fact, about a month ago I committed to becoming a follower of the King, and I also received an invitation to go to Remiah. Zoe, think about it—it was our maps, which were designed by the King that led us to each other! He planned this all along! I have been waiting for the right time to tell you about my journey—and now I find that you are going to Remiah too!"

It was astonishing—they both set out on a journey, for different reasons, but ultimately it was their journeys that enabled them to find each other.

Zoe stood up and hugged her mother. "I could not be happier! Please, could I see your map?"

They compared their maps, and though their origination points were different, their maps were the same from where they were now, to their destination point of Remiah!

Zoe hugged her mother again. "This is so wonderful that we can go to Remiah together. I am in awe of the King for planning something so incredible for the both of us. Tell me, how did you come to know the King?"

Mary smiled. "One day I was sewing where I worked—"

"I don't mean to interrupt you, but are you telling me that you're a seamstress?"

"Well, yes. About ten years ago, I took a position in a small tailor shop in my village and Mrs. Venita taught me how to sew."

"This is amazing. I, too, am a seamstress!"

"Oh my! This is hard to believe."

"I was thinking the same thing. I'm sorry I interrupted your story. Please, go on."

"I was busy sewing a gown when one of the other seamstresses began sharing about the King. I could not believe I had never heard about Him before. She had a copy of the King's Book and she brought it to the shop that day. I asked her if I could read it when we had our meal at noon. She told me that I could. Well, I read for thirty minutes, not even taking a bite of my scone. The Words seemed to jump off the pages and into my heart. I have never read any Words so moving, and I knew it was all true. I talked more to my friend after work, and she told me how I could know the King myself. It was then that I became His follower."

"Soon after that, a messenger came to the shop and gave me this invitation." She handed it to Zoe.

"What was the name of this messenger?"

"Kieran."

Zoe had to sit down. "He is the same messenger who delivered my invitation to me!"

"This is so amazing—it was all orchestrated by the King! I had a burning desire in my heart to find you, which was placed there by the King. Now I find our chosen paths are leading us to Remiah together!"

"This just confirms to me that if we are truly following the King, He will lead us down the right path, our true heart's desire—the one He intended for us all along."

Mary studied Zoe, her expression thoughtful. "Well then, I say it's time to pack up and go to Remiah!"

Brogan was excited. He kept running ahead and coming back with his tail wagging. Mary and Zoe caught on to his excitement and energetically pushed forward at a faster pace. After they had walked half a day on the road, Remiah was in clear view. The mountain was dense with thick evergreen trees which stood very tall. There were many rocky cliffs, but there was a path that led through them clearly to the top.

Toward evening they decided to stop at the foot of the mountain. Brogan had gone ahead to find a suitable place for them to stay the night. He returned and said that there was a small cottage nearby. "Nobody lives there, yet it looks clean and will make a nice shelter for the night. There is a fireplace and plenty of firewood stacked outside."

Zoe commended her friend. "Excellent, Brogan. Lead the way."

As they approached the little cottage, they noticed wildflowers blooming everywhere, with a nice stone walkway leading up to the front door. They walked inside and were quite pleased. Zoe thought that surely the King must keep this cottage to bless all those who have almost reached their journey's end of Remiah.

"Zoe, rest a little while and I'll prepare our meal."

Zoe smiled and thought how wonderful it was to have her mother care for her again. "Thank you. I believe I will," as she closed her eyes in perfect peace.

Mary found some fresh apples on a tree nearby and laid them out with the food left from what Jenna and Arden had sent. Zoe soon awoke and they all ate until they were full. She read the King's Book to them and then they visited until everyone became so sleepy they decided to go to bed. They laid their pallets on the floor and slept by the fire.

As the morning sun shone through the one window in their haven for the night, Zoe reflected upon what this day might bring. Soon she would be in Remiah, and she could not wait to see the King again. She began to get very excited and woke Mary and Brogan. "Mother, it's a beautiful day—today we see the King!"

Mary turned over and tried to close her eyes again until she fully realized what Zoe had just said. She sat straight up. "Zoe, you just called me *Mother*."

"So I did. You are my Mother, are you not?" Zoe grinned.

Her face lit up with pleasure. "Yes, I am. And, it is a beautiful day! I get to be with my precious daughter today *and* see the King! How could the day be any better?"

"I am happy to be with you too, so let's hurry and eat and be on our way."

Brogan slowly stood, stretched, and caught on to the excitement. His tail was wagging and he, too, wholeheartedly agreed that they needed to be on their way.

So they ate, packed, grabbed some berries from the bush outside the cottage, and headed toward the path up the mountain. The incline became very steep and Mary lost her footing once, sliding down about ten feet, but she soon learned how to walk more carefully. They reached an area that was fairly level so they decided to rest for a few minutes.

As Zoe looked around she realized they were at the very gate to the city of the King! Everyone became excited until Zoe sat down and felt the keys that were in her pocket, and pulled out only one key. Frantically, she looked around. *Where are the other keys? Did I drop them?* When she looked closely, this key was entirely different than the others. It was still gold, but it was outlined in red rubies, and it was much larger. It had an inscription in very small letters that said: **Peace, Faithfulness, Patience, Self-control, Kindness, Goodness, Gentleness**, and *Joy* and in large letters was the word **LOVE**. All the keys had become one!

A stranger suddenly approached them. He was handsome and walked with a confident gait.

"Have you come to the city of the King?" Before they could answer, he said, "I'm here to help you prepare to meet Him. There is a certain, definite protocol here you know, which you must not violate."

Zoe felt uncomfortable. There was something too confident about this man. He somehow exuded a subtle arrogance, and she had never felt that about any of the King's messengers before.

"Now, please," the stranger said, extending his hand, "Let me see the key you have."

Zoe gazed at the stranger, feeling more like protecting the key than giving it to him. She also felt like protecting her mother and Brogan, so she stepped in front of them as if to shield them.

The stranger continued, "For you to have gone this far you must have the key of **LOVE**, and love 'believes all things.' Love is trusting. I must examine the key of everyone who enters here and you are making me think that you do not have the right key."

"It seems to me that you are the one who is not trusting," Zoe shot right back, discerning that he was definitely not one of the King's messengers. "I will not let you touch the key or anything else that I have."

The stranger immediately transformed into Durgalt himself. His dark eyes were breathing fire now. "So you thought that you of all people would actually make it to the city of the King? How foolish...how naive...I rule all of the territory around His city and no one passes through this gate or any gate without my permission. You fool, you should have stayed in your little cottage and then I would have left you alone. Now I'm going to have fun with you and your pitiful friends."

"You will not," Zoe fired back, drawing her bow and aiming directly at his chest.

He laughed hideously. She fired. Durgalt did not flinch as the arrow disintegrated. "Go ahead. Shoot them all. They are useless anyway." Then Durgalt inched closer. Zoe stood her ground. For a split second she saw doubt, maybe even fear, flash across his face.

"Give me the key and I will let you return to your cottage and live. I will even let your friends live."

"You don't have the power to tell me whether I can live or not. You don't have the power to keep me from using this key to enter through that gate. Zoe took a step toward Durgalt and then she was certain she saw fear in his eyes.

His eyes manifested more evil than she had ever seen before. She held her ground. With a foulness that surrounded him, he spewed out, "Do not come any closer. You cannot enter through that gate! I have more power than you could ever imagine. Stop!"

Zoe continued walking forward without wavering. Now Durgalt began to back up, stumbling out of her way. She reached in her pocket for the key to open the gate, and Durgalt reached out his hand to grab Mary. "Don't." Zoe said, opening the gate. Durgalt backed up. "Be gone in the name of the King." Astonished, he could do nothing but vanish for he no longer had any power over her.

Kieran appeared in an almost blinding array of light and color such as they had never seen. Mary fell on her knees. Brogan and Zoe were likewise awed, but stood motionless.

"Please stand," Kieran said, "Taking Mary's hand and lifting her to her feet. "I am your servant."

"Well done, Zoe," he said as he bowed to her. "The King has sent me to escort you into His court where the celebration is to begin."

"What celebration is that?" Zoe asked, still awed by the glory of Kieran's presence.

"The celebration of your victory. All of heaven is rejoicing over you and your companions. You have learned the King's ways. You have resisted the evil one. You have the key. It is yours and if you do not willingly surrender it, no power can ever take it from you. Now you have the authority to sit with the King and rule with Him. He has a special place prepared for you—an eternal seat in the court of the King. I am your servant, as is all the host of heaven at your service now," he said, again bowing low.

Mary was speechless. She still felt like falling to the ground in homage. Kieran seemed to sense this, and turned to her, bowing.

"Mary, you too have overcome. You are greatly loved and honored in the household of the King. Look in your pocket. You also have the key."

Mary reached into her pocket and pulled out a key just like Zoe's key. Marveling, she stammered, "How could this be? I have not done anything like Zoe. She crossed through the wilderness, the desert, fought in the great war, and much more. I just began the journey, and I would not have even made it the little bit that I traveled, much less gotten past that evil creature who was just here, if it had not been for Zoe. I don't deserve anything."

"Mary, you have been on this journey your whole life. You learned the two great graces, love and humility, a long time ago. It was these that enabled you to resist going to find your daughter and taking her back. You died to your own desires every day so she could have a better life. You never walked in selfishness, and you suffered much at the hands of others without becoming bitter. That is why, when the invitation was given, your journey was so short and seemingly easy compared to Zoe's. You have always been close to the kingdom, you just did not know it. Mary, you are greatly loved, and greatly esteemed by the entire host of heaven."

Kieran again bowed to Mary, "The King is most pleased with you, Mary. You are one of the faithful ones, and you have walked in the way of love though few have understood it. Your authority in heaven is great. You have an honored seat at the King's table. He has been waiting a long time for you, as have we all. I know it is still hard for you to believe, but I will not need to repeat it again, you will soon see for yourself."

Zoe could hardly contain her joy as they walked through the gate. As they passed, Kieran turned to Brogan. "You are a faithful friend. You have been through the same trials as Zoe, so you will receive your reward in full—you too will enter into the King's house. The companions of the holy ones will all join you here. You will be surprised at how many of your ancestors are waiting to greet you."

Brogan wagged his tail profusely. "Thank you!"

As they passed through the gates, the glory that enveloped them nearly took their breath away. The road to the King's palace was lined with messengers as brilliant as Kieran, all standing at attention with swords raised in salute. In all of their dreams they had never even imagined such a glorious spectacle. This was truly beyond anyone's imagination to behold. They walked slowly, wanting to take it all in. Their minds and thoughts became brilliant and more clear than they had ever conceived. It was as if their minds had emerged from a dungeon into a clear blue day. The feeling was more wonderful than they ever thought possible.

The walk now seemed effortless, even up the steep incline to the King's palace. There was new joy and new glory in every step they took. They soon understood it was because they were getting closer to the King, for He is the Light.

Zoe smelled the fragrance that permeated the air. "The air has never been this clean, this clear. The bushes, trees, and flowers have no dead growth on them—they are perfect in every way. I have never seen such green leaves. Everything looks so healthy."

The messenger said, "There is no death in the presence of our King. You will find that all of the colors on earth are deeply faded and few. There are many more colors here than you have seen before. The air is pure because there is no death and no evil here. There is only life."

Mary's face lit up with joy. "Zoe, I feel wonderful. I'm not tired anymore. Look at Brogan. All of his wounds are healed completely and he is as frisky as a puppy."

The ascent was so spectacular that Zoe and Mary wanted to stop and look at everything. Every imaginable flower was in its healthiest state, and their colors were breathtaking. The vegetable gardens were perfect, and in the neatest rows Zoe had ever seen. No disease was found anywhere. They could only stand and look in awe at the King's handiwork.

The grass was bright green with no weeds anywhere. The trees swayed with the warm breath of fresh air, and birds were singing sweet songs of praise to the King. They could see lions, tigers, goats, and lambs playing together. Kittens were playing with large dogs, who obviously took great delight in the little ones. Peace and unity ruled everywhere.

"Look Mother, Brogan! In the distance over the hill, do you see the King's palace? This is more wonderful than any dream could ever be! Just think, we are about to see the King in His glory! Let's hurry!"

The messenger said, "There is no need to hurry for you will arrive at just the right time. You will find that everything is perfect here."

"For the gate is small, and the way is narrow that leads to life, and few are those who find it."
Matthew 7:14

Chapter Thirty

*I have fought the good fight, I have finished the course,
I have kept the faith.
II Timothy 4:7*

Zoe's heart was racing as they approached the entrance to the palace. After all that she had been through it was hard for her to believe that she had finally made it to Remiah. Since passing through the outer gate their vision had and was still increasing dramatically. They were all seeing colors with a richness and depth they had never seen before.

"Mother, look—your gown has changed and you look so beautiful! The color is the most exquisite emerald green I have ever seen," Zoe exclaimed, almost breathless with excitement. Mary looked down at her dress and was amazed to see she did have a new gown and that it was her favorite color.

"Zoe, look at your gown!" It was no longer pale and worn, but was now a deep, rich, purple and absolutely perfect for her. "Your face is glowing! You look so beautiful!" Zoe gazed at her dress, stunned. She had never felt so elegant in all her life. For a couple of seamstresses who had a special love for fine clothes, but who could never afford them, this made them feel that they had certainly entered into heaven itself.

Kieran smiled. "Your clothing here is a reflection of your desire, an outpouring of creativity deep within you."

As they walked, their eyes opened more and more, and so did their minds. This was the only way they had the capacity to see the glory, and to experience the joy. As Zoe looked down at Brogan it was obvious that the same thing was happening to him.

Then they all felt the presence of the King. Zoe turned, and then gasped when she saw Him. He was even more majestic now that their eyes were open to see Him in more fullness of His glory. They all stood speechless as He approached them. They could not help but bow low before Him. Even the angels paled in comparison to His glory.

"You have done well My good and faithful servants! Now there is much for you to see here. Follow Me."

When they walked through His garden, Mary, Zoe, and even Brogan were overwhelmed by what they saw. The beauty and fullness of the plants were truly heavenly for there was simply nothing like them on earth. Soon tears were streaming from Zoe and Mary's eyes as they felt love from and for everything they saw. Then they saw nine healthy, beautiful trees, plentiful with unique kinds of brightly colored ripe fruit. Each of the tree's names was engraved in gold. When Zoe looked closer, she could not believe her eyes! The first and largest tree in the garden was engraved *LOVE*. The second tree was *Joy*. The next was *Peace, Patience, Gentleness, Kindness, Goodness, Faithfulness,* and *Self-Control.*

"My King, these trees have the very names of the keys I acquired on my journey!"

"Yes, Zoe. This is why the trees are so special to Me. They bear the fruit from every lesson learned by those who make the journey to My kingdom. Now you may eat the fruit of your labor! Each bite you take will enable the seed that has already been planted within you to grow and ripen into full maturity."

Zoe and Mary ate from the *Tree of LOVE* first because this was the key that had been the most difficult to acquire. The fruit melted in their mouths, and the sweetness of love began to permeate into their whole being.

The King turned to Brogan. "Go ahead—help yourself to the fruit too."

Brogan ate and looked at the King with gratitude. They took their time and ate from every tree. Each one was a different fruit having its own unique flavor, leaving a different effect within them. After eating from each tree, all of the fruit seemed to merge into a deep love, which gave them the desire to help others, and a feeling of confidence and strength that they could.

When they finished eating and were walking with the King, He began to speak to them again. "You have partaken of the fruit of the Spirit. He is called the Helper. When you eat the true fruit that can only grow in the lives of those who live in My kingdom, the result is that you take on His nature as the Helper. You want to help everyone you can. It is in Him that you are also given the strength and wisdom to succeed."

"My King, I have never felt so fulfilled as I do at this very moment. I am bursting with love for You. In one way I want to stay here forever, but in another way, I want to go back and help those who so desperately need what we have found. It's hard to choose what to do."

"My little Princess, you do not have to choose between them. Now that you have come to My kingdom you can live here forever. You can even live here while you return to fulfill your purpose with the strength of the Helper. Now you are in this city, but when you leave, the city will be in you, and you will forever be a resident.

"The Spirit and I are one. These fruits of **LOVE**, **Joy**, **Peace**, **Patience**, **Gentleness**, **Kindness**, **Goodness**, **Faithfulness**, and **Self-Control.** are what **I AM**! They will continue to grow within you because you are growing into Me. You are becoming like Me. When you finish your purpose on the earth, which is the rest of your journey, you will be with Me forever. The more of these fruits that grow within you, the closer you will be seated to My throne. Let this fruit continue to grow. Cultivate the garden of your heart, and plant seeds in others that they too may grow. You plant seeds by your acts of love for others.

"You must also learn to come often to eat fruit from these trees. Each time you are able to give a little more love to someone else, love will grow deeper within you. The same is true with each fruit.

"I must also give you a warning. There are many people who come to know Me who do not ever make it here. There are others who make it here but do not go on to fulfill their purpose on the earth. You have made it here because you learned to stay on the path of life, your chosen path, which is to walk in wisdom and the fruit of the Spirit. You have learned to recognize and resist the evil one and the fruit of evil that is in the world. Even so, you must not think that you cannot be distracted or misled again.

"Some of your coming trials will be even more difficult because your maturity will cause the evil one to view you as a much greater threat, and he will therefore send his strongest and best to stop you. This is allowed so that you can defeat them and set even more people free from his powers of darkness. The bigger battles ahead only mean the greater your victory will be, and the greater the numbers who are helped by you.

"You have learned the joys of My love, My peace, and the ecstasy of worship, but you must never forget that you are a warrior too. I love every soul on the earth, even those who hate Me now. For each one that comes, My kingdom gets a little larger on the earth, My light shines brighter, and more will therefore be able to come to Me here.

"I could have come to you and brought you here immediately after you gave your heart to Me. However, if it had not been for your journey and all that you learned, you would not have the fruit in your life nor would you be the great Princess warrior and deliverer that you are now. The journey to My kingdom is not meant to be easy—it is meant to be effective in forming those who will reign with Me forever.

"Now you must go back into the enemy's kingdom. His entire host knows you now, and they will fight you in everything you do. They will try to find any weakness in you, and they will find some and hurt you there. This can help you even more if you acknowledge your weaknesses and seek My grace for them. Then they will make you even stronger. But do not ever think that you cannot fall or cannot be tricked by the evil ones, for then you are certain to fall and be deceived. When you fulfill your destiny, you become more humble."

The words of the King were received as sober truth by Zoe, Mary, and Brogan. They all began to understand that this was not the end of their journey, but the beginning. This desire to help others was growing much stronger in them. As much as they loved being in the presence of the King, at the same time they were filled with a desire to go back and help the King's servants, to free those in bondage to the evil one.

The King looked deeply into their eyes. "You will fight in the battles of the last days. These will be the biggest battles ever. The fruit that you have received here are your weapons. You will be successful and given power in proportion to the fruit that grows in you."

Zoe and Mary bowed before the King. Zoe looked straight into the His eyes and saw the depth of His love for her. She could not contain her love for Him. At last she spoke. "No one has ever served a more noble King or a more noble cause. Eternity will not be long enough to thank You for what You have done for us. Thank You for this call. We will seek to do all that You ask, and to help all that we can to know You. No one could ever be more blessed than to be a subject of Yours, and to live in Your realm. We want to be worthy warriors of Your kingdom, and help all to see the truth of who You are. There certainly could never be a more noble purpose, and we are overwhelmed with gratitude to have been given this honor."

Both Zoe and Mary wanted to embrace the King more than ever because they were so filled with love for Him. At the same time He was so awesome that they were a bit reticent. They both cried with joy as He took them and drew them into an embrace. He touched their cheeks and stroked their hair with such tenderness and love that they knew everything they had been through in their lives was worth this one moment. Then He reached down and stroked Brogan's chin, stood up, and took Zoe and Mary by the hand and walked with them into the palace.

"Once the entrance is made into My kingdom, the door always remains open for you. You have the key. It is the same key that brings you into My chambers. You can be as close to Me as you want to be. This is the special place where we will share everything. This is where you will truly learn the things of My heart, and you will share your deepest thoughts with Me. Come often. I am always here waiting for you. This is your home too."

The three did not know how long they had been in the King's chambers, but in a very profound way they felt that this house was theirs. It was everything that they desired, and everything was just as they would have made it in their dreams. It was as wonderful as the garden, only very different. It was where they belonged. It was "home" if there ever was a place that could truly describe that word.

It was during this time that the King also began to talk to them about the great treasures that were hidden on the earth, and the many that the evil one had found and hidden so that no one would ever find them again. To their amazement, the King said one of their main purposes now was to find some of these treasures so that they might be returned to His house. Just talking about these treasures awakened a great and wonderful intrigue in their hearts.

Mary said, "Lord, just talking about this makes me feel the same way I did when reading the great fairy tales."

"Mary, this is no fairly tale, but these treasures have been given to mankind alone, and there is a yearning for them in the heart of every soul on the earth. This yearning comes forth in many dreams and tales, so there is truth in them, but you are not to follow tales. You are called to follow Me. I will lead you to the treasures you are to find."

All of this resulted in filling them each with a purpose so great that in spite of the joy they were experiencing, which was far beyond anything they had ever experienced before, they all started to feel a yearning to begin—to help those who were in need of their help. The King, observing this, finally drew them all close to Him. Mary and Brogan were at His feet, and Zoe leaned against Him. He smiled while looking deeply into the eyes of each, and then He simply said, "It is now time for your to return. Close your eyes."

⟶✳⟵

When she opened her eyes, Zoe knew exactly where they were—Runden Forest. King Ronan was not far away. As the three began to walk toward him, he greeted them with great joy. "Why Zoe! You're back. Welcome!"

"Oh, King Ronan, it's so good to be back and so good to see you!"

"It's wonderful to see you again too my dear. And welcome to you, Brogan. I am very glad to see you again, too."

"Thank you, and it is a pleasure to be here."

Zoe restlessly looked around for Arden. King Ronan answered her thoughts.

"Arden is by the river my dear. Go to him."

Zoe smiled and ran to find him. Then she quickly turned around, realizing that she had not introduced her mother to King Ronan. "Oh, please forgive me. This is my mother, Mary, King Ronan." They were already staring at each other.

"Mother, this is King Ronan."

He took her hands and gazed deeply into her eyes. "Welcome to Runden Forest, m'lady."

As Zoe was running to the river, she turned back and said, "Please excuse me. I must find Arden."

"Go my daughter. He has been anxiously awaiting your return."

King Ronan turned back to Mary and she curtsied. "Thank you, King Ronan. It is a pleasure to meet you."

"The pleasure and honor is all mine. Would you care to take a walk with me?"

"I would be most pleased to do so. I have heard so much about your realm, and I had hoped one day to see it. I just never dreamed that the king himself would show it to me!" He took one of her hands and placed it in his arm.

At last Zoe saw Prince Arden. Moments passed after their eyes met, and then suddenly, she saw and felt the depth of his love. She ran to him and he quickly enclosed her in his arms. He held her for a long time, never wanting to let her go again. When they finally released each other, Arden gazed into her eyes. "You have returned to me! I missed you more than words can say. But you have changed my Princess. I never thought you could be any more beautiful than when last I saw you, but you are! There is a new glow about you."

An intense emotion arose from deep within Zoe. It was something she had never felt before. "I have just returned from Remiah. We made it Arden. We have been with the King! It was the most amazing experience of my life, and more wonderful than anything on this earth—far more! I now know what has been missing in my life, and between us Arden. I have something to tell you."

The depth of her heart was revealed when she whispered simply, "I love you."

He lifted her face to touch his, and kissed her with all of the love that had been held back for this very moment. When the warmth of the kiss ended, she gazed into her Prince's eyes, knowing that she truly loved him. She was ready to fulfill her role as Princess and begin a new journey with Arden. At last she knew how to love for she had been taught by the One who best knew how to love— her King.

That evening King Ronan, Mary, Prince Arden, Zoe, and Brogan stood watching the sunset from a cliff overlooking a land that went as far as the eye could see. They all stood silently, thinking of the future. Though they did not speak, they were all thinking the same thing. There was a destiny that awaited them far away. There were treasures to be found. It would be both dangerous and wonderful, and they all felt that these treasures were actually calling them, beckoning them to even greater discoveries. Soon they would share their thoughts with each other, and soon another journey would have to begin.

"Well done, good and faithful servant!
you have been faithful with a few things;
I will put you in charge of many things.
Come and share your master's happiness!"
Matthew 25:21 (NIV)

For a **free**
catalog of other books
and materials by
MorningStar,
please call
1-800-542-0278